LIBRARY OF TIME

A MAGE BORN LIBRARIAN AND SEER CLAIMS A MYSTERIOUS LEGACY

RIA LOADER

IMPISH PRESS
SHORELINE, WA, USA 2015

Impish Press
PO Box 65198
Shoreline, Washington 98155
www.impishpress.com

Publisher's Note: This is a work of fiction. Names, characters, places, and incidents are a product of the author's imagination. Locales and public names are sometimes used for atmospheric purposes. Any resemblance to actual people, living or dead, or to businesses, companies, events, institutions, or locales is completely coincidental.

Book Cover Design—Ria Loader

Ria Loader Author / Urban Fantasy, Adventure, Portals and Gates, Mages and Magic, Books and Libraries

Library of Time/ Ria Loader -- 1st ed.
ISBN 978-0-6923743-4-4

CONTENTS

DEDICATION

To my mother and father for always believing in me, and for sharing a love of books and stories. Thanks for being such terrific parents and for encouraging creativity, self-reliance and kindness.

ACKNOWLEDGEMENTS

Many thanks to my beta readers for making the story better —with special thanks to Bill, Colleen, Dominic, Dawn and Liam. With gratitude and love to Raven, for he is the best alpha reader and partner that a writer could have; he was a constant sounding board and inspiration during the development of the world and the story.

I'd like to thank the Jewel Box cafe and staff in Seattle where much of this novel was written. I also owe a big thanks to Nanowrimo for getting me into the habit of writing every day. I shouldn't forget the writers who inspire me, and they are many . . . and the musicians who make the soundtrack of life. Special thanks to S J Tucker for her knack for telling stories with music.

SUZZALO ANNEX, SEATTLE

Present Day

It was twilight in the Suzzalo library annex in downtown Seattle. Late summer light slanted through the high windows, making patterns across the worn, dappled oak beams of the floor. The stillness of the air in the corridors held an impression of the people who had passed through, stayed for a while, and then departed with their borrowed books. Hints of cologne and wet wool lingered after the latest in a series of uncommon thunderstorms. Fall was approaching along with the colicky weather, still, September in Seattle held the last blessings of summer.

The furthest reaches of the library were seldom visited, filled as they were with dusty tomes. Those older sections of the library gathered chronons, time particles that slid into the spaces between books, rubbing shoulders with the dust motes from ancient manuscripts. All old things gathered time particles and impressions, though books seemed predisposed to store more time energy than most objects. Mira could feel the chronons stirring now and then, reaching out beyond the shelves to twine around her legs like a playful and invisible fog. Mira had always been sensitive to time, likely something she had inherited from her odd family. All her family tangled with time in one way or another.

She closed down the reference desk for the day, locking the cabinets with the precious collection of mono prints and hand-bound books. The mono prints included singular pieces of book binding from the print studio at Cornish College of the Arts, one-of-a-kind pieces of art. She always felt like locking the cabinets added a layer of protection to their care. She couldn't resist sketching a charm of protection, more for her own comfort than from any real sense of danger to the beautiful volumes.

Some of the valuable treasures were rare examples of creative book-binding, with hand-set letters, lovingly crafted. Others were examples of small press editions of esoteric works, like medieval grimoires, or treatises on alchemy. Mixed in with them were folios of rare prints. There was even a first edition print from Austin Osman Spare in a leather-bound folio.

She had to admit to feeling itchy and restless, as if the energy of the storm had wandered inside the library and taken up residence just beneath her breast-bone. It was not an unfamiliar feeling of late. Something was going to change soon, she felt it keenly. And though she was part of it, she could not see the shape of the pattern clearly.

She'd been sleeping less and dreaming more in recent months. The dreams were jumbled, almost like the odd dreams she had as a child. The images in those dreams belonged more to books of fairy tales, or to stories of elder gods. She thought she'd left all that behind her when she moved to the city as a college freshman. Mira had deliberately sought the Quiet Way, a discipline from her magical training with Gran, to make it easier for her to fit in with her college friends.

It seemed she'd been mistaken in her assumptions of continued normalcy. She hoped that the other kinds of oddness were not going to follow the strange dreams. It wasn't yet the season for whimsy or the stirring of enchantments. The season for those things would come in another month or so, closer to Hallows.

She had worked hard at establishing a practical and reliable reputation as a research librarian, so she muttered a charm against the sight under her breath, just like Gran would have done. It may keep her unruly talent for seeing the true nature of things under control. She reminded herself of Gran's old saying 'If you don't look with the sight, the twilight world is less likely to notice you back'. If wishing could make it so, then wishing is what she would do. It did feel a little like she was acting like a small child, though, ignoring a monster under the bed. It was not a comfortable feeling. Mira sneezed suddenly. Magic was stirring, and it did odd things to her sinuses.

The ways of magic were second-nature to her having grown up with magical beings as playmates. Nowadays though, she used her magic absently, striving to live in the moment in the normal world she had chosen for herself. There were enough events and fellow travelers to meet here in the Middle Kingdom without bringing the world of waking dream into every day consideration. Still, it was not always easy to deny that part of herself. She allowed herself the charms and the deflections, the spells of peace and calm, and the small magics to ease her way. She felt that the small things she did to guide true seekers to the books they needed, occasionally matching up students with likely teachers, was being true to herself without her reaching out for too much prominence.

Mira loved researching civilizations, and being able to go on the occasional archeological dig with college buddies filled her with a quiet satisfaction. As a librarian, she was a kind of caretaker and knowledge trader, a maker of patterns. If now and then those patterns rather resembled magical cantrips, well then that was all right too.

Once in a while she ran into beings who were Other. They, however, often failed to recognize her for what she was, another magical being like themselves. Though Mira was of mixed blood, that was common enough nowadays, and nothing to remark upon. She had deliberately worn a glamor, here in the world of her own library, to avoid anyone noticing her. Their glances slid aside, and their energy touched her only a little in passing.

There were a couple of friends she kept up with from her Gran's magical worlds. However, those friends were mostly from her father's family. Keeping up with family was a survival characteristic given their dabbling in politics and power. It was also good to keep up with the family gossip via those few members she considered friends. She also liked to drop in to the family place in Portland occasionally, to playfully upset their power plays. It was a childish habit, she'd admit. She guessed she got her mischievous nature from growing up with her grandmother in a world of magic.

2

ENTRANCES AND EXITS

Mira briskly shook off her thoughts and moved towards the front door, ready to close the rest of the library for the day.

Just then, a bedraggled and diffident young man stumbled through the door. A sense of power entered with him, making questionable his mild appearance.

"Sorry, sorry" he said to the air around him, as he came through the door. He managed to snag his coat, trip over the door rim and run into the coat rack, more or less at the same time. That was quite a trick given that those items were about three feet apart. His hands were restless, in turn taking off a battered fedora, smoothing back his wet dark hair, straightening his worn, long woolen jacket. He pushed his old-fashioned horned-rimmed glasses up his nose, with fluttering fingers. Long hands she noticed with elegant fingers, though slightly mottled now with the unexpected cold and rain.

"Late. Sorry. Looking for a book," he said, sounding like an old recording, or like someone too distracted to pay attention to the social niceties.

"You've come to the right place, then." She made her tone soothing, hoping that would help. "The library has many books."

"Oh!" he exclaimed, recalling himself. "Yes, of course. But I meant . . . let me start over."

He straightened up, took a deep breath and centered himself, becoming suddenly a point of stillness in the dusty light of the foyer.

"It is a particular book I am looking for," he said seriously. "The Rede of Trees." He glanced over at her hopefully. "Your Gran sent me."

Well he looked interesting enough, if a bit mad. Gran had been dead, or something quite like dead, for the past five years.

"You are a bit late, aren't you?" Mira asked, with a smile in her voice. She gazed at him in bemusement. "Just let me lock up. We'll chat over a nice cuppa tea".

Even if Seattle folks usually preferred coffee, when a stray with his odd energy wandered into her library asking for Gran's book, it was definitely time for a proper cup of tea.

Mira took a last look around, to see that there were no lingering students in the study carrels or quietly browsing in the stacks. She went to the front door, turned over the closed sign, latched and locked the front door securely.

"Hang up your coat over there," she said, waving her arm in the direction of the coat rack he had collided with earlier. "Don't want water all over."

She watched the start of another flutter of confusion from him as he shook out his coat and tripped over it on the way to the coat rack. Suppressing her laughter, she headed for the private staff room. She was the last one here today and very grateful for it. There would be no interruptions while she worked out what to do with him.

As she walked away, she spoke over her shoulder.

"This way to the staff room" she said, expecting that he would follow her.

Looking a little bemused after his epic battle with the coat, he shrugged, reaching out towards the rack to hang up the rain-soaked jacket.

"Do come along when you're ready," she added.

When she reached the staff room, all the way to the back and to the left hand side of the corridor, she opened the door, leaving it that way. No sense in making it hard for him to find, she thought.

Mira briskly walked across to the bench under the window, and moved a stack of books from the straight-backed chair at the scuffed table. She ran her hands over her head to check if it was as messy as usual. It was, of course. She sighed. A habit she shared with her mother was a tendency to clutch at her head while thinking. It made a real mess of the long, dark blond mass of it. She'd also stuck a pencil in it to twist it up off her neck. Another bad habit. Well at least it wasn't a paintbrush as her mother frequently displayed, complete with colored paint.

Checking the mirror over the kettle, she wiped a smudge off her tawny nose. She quite liked her features, and her nose was well shaped she thought. Her favorite feature though was her slightly larger-than-normal eyes. Anime eyes, her friends called them. Mira re-twisted her hair with a proper hair stick this time. Presentable mixed-race features, direct green eyes with no makeup, chewed off lip gloss, hair mostly tidy. Well enough. That would do. It was a customary check whenever she went to make tea. If she didn't check, she'd soon look as chaotic as her mother, though not half as pretty.

Turning on the ancient electric kettle her capable hands automatically moved through the ritual steps of rinsing out a favorite silver tea pot at the corner sink. Then she reached for some mismatched tea cups.

She measured tea leaves into the pot, then set out some home-made shortbread along with chocolate cookies on a blue-and-white china plate. The tiny refrigerator yielded some cream in a small jug and a plastic container with lemon wedges.

She leaned her medium–height, lanky form casually against a bench, just in time to watch him as he reached the doorway. The room seemed to shift a bit as he entered, shadows gathering in the corners. She gestured to the chair, and took a quick breath as he shook his head, and straightened to a ridiculously tall six feet four or more. He was immediately a much more definite person, though he did manage to hit his shoulder on the way into the room. His air of purpose was not matched by any grace. He was as improbable and clumsy a being as she'd seen in a while.

Mira hoped she had not made a mistake in being alone with a stranger. She did have some resources to deal with mistakes, should it come to that, among which was more than a few years of martial discipline. She reached out her hand as she offered an informal greeting.

"Hi, I'm Mira," she said. "And you must be?"

She waited for him to introduce himself, albeit belatedly. She never could get normal social stuff in the right order. She'd already berated him for being late, without actually knowing his name.

He grinned, with a closed mouth and laughing eyes and firmly clasped hands with her. The goofy grin made him look friendly again, though she wasn't going to forget that moment of hard focus, nor the sense of a heavy ancient power that seemed to surround him like invisible smoke.

"Edward," he said.

"Not a sparkly kind of vampire then?" she quipped out loud, resorting to humor.

"No. Not that kind..." He paused. "Eleison. Edward Eleison. Did your grandmother tell you about me?"

"Not as such," Mira replied. "But I've been expecting someone like you to turn up." The kettle made a distinctive click, letting her know the water had boiled.

"Just a sec," she said, "while I make us some tea."

She was a little surprised at herself, taking the notion of him in stride. He was just the kind of surprise she ought to have expected, given her dreams. He was clearly not accustomed to his current body, and that said to her that it was a new form he was wearing. She rather wondered what form he had worn before turning into a real boy. Whatever it was she sensed, it was ancient and powerful. However, she wasn't going to give in to curiosity and peek at his aura to find out what his Other shape was. Waiting until after tea would be quite soon enough for that.

Mira carefully poured water into the silver teapot. She took a breath, blessed the tea deva, and ritually turned the tea pot three times, clockwise, to set a spell of friendship on it. An everyday enchantment was a good balance for the rather less-than-everyday being occupying the break room.

"Please, join me." she said, taking her usual seat, directly opposite the one she'd cleared for him. "Lemon for you?" she asked. She added it as he nodded agreement. She poured the tea, taking solace from the familiar motions.

While they stepped through the ritual of silently appreciating the tea, she mused to herself about Gran's book. A while back, Gran had talked her into taking custody of part of her Library. Gran had been feeling tired, she said to Mira, and needed to confuse her trail for a bit.

Argent Astra had been a bossy old woman who attracted trouble her entire life, or was that lives, Mira wondered. Though ancient, Gran had never appeared to look a day over thirty. She was the very maven of style and culture. If Gran said she needed to confound her enemies, though, Mira was happy to help her. The book was her most precious possession, Gran had said.

Calling it a book was a bit of misdirection though. It was more like a whole Library tesseracted into a book. The book itself was compacted even further into a spell. The whole thing was called the Rede of Trees.

Mira hadn't figured on the Rede needing to be carried quite so close, let alone inked on her body. It seemed like a strange way to look after something from Gran's Library. Yet Gran said it would hide it from harm to do it that way.

Gran had promised her she would send someone for the Rede. However that was before she disappeared and for all practical purposes in this world, died. Though there were no bodily remains, Gran had dissolved into light, and by her own Wishing.

Mira had mixed feelings about Gran being gone from the world. With Others, it was often confusing when they changed shape. The person who cared for them never knew if they'd show up in a new form in five years, fifty years or even five hundred. It depended on where they departed to.

Some places didn't keep the same time as the world. For all intents and purposes though, Gran was gone and Mira mourned her loss as a personal tragedy. At the same time, she would not be at all surprised to see her looking out of the eyes of a new body. If that happened, then she'd put aside grief. In the meantime, however, she tried to think about Gran as absent, rather than gone.

The Rede of Trees was likely to get Mira into trouble in the meantime. She would need help with the magic required to transfer the Rede to a more permanent location than a fragile human, well mostly-human, body. It was only her mixed blood that allowed her to carry it at all, artifact that it was.

It must have been the book whispering, causing the dreams, she thought. Now, if this man was Gran's promised emissary, she'd be happy to get it out of her body and back into a proper magical library; though she supposed it could be worked again into an artifact, or even stored in a Dragon Hoard. It needed to be safer than she could make it on her own, should anyone think she was carrying it.

"So, about this particular book?" she asked gently.

"You have it here in the Library?" he asked urgently. "It's here? We need to get it and leave. It can't fall into the wrong hands."

"Drink your tea. Try a cookie," she said, just to see his reaction to eating the rich dark chocolate. How he reacted to chocolate would tell her something about what kind of Other he might be. The different races seemed to have such interesting tells as the alkaloids in the chocolate affected them all so differently.

"Tell me about Gran sending you." She needed to decide if he was part of Gran's problem, or if he was the messenger who she said would come.

"Tea. Right," he said, taking a sip, then a longer one, draining the cup. He did not seem to notice it was too hot to swig down that fast. She was quickly forming an opinion about his true shape. He quickly munched a cookie, saying "good" between bites.

"There that's done." He seemed to settle into himself as he looked down at his hands, twisting them into a complex pattern. When he looked up, his eyes had changed color to a darker gold than the friendly, mild brown they'd been when she first saw him. His nature seemed somewhat mercurial, shifting from one moment to the next, from diffident young man to ancient being hiding his form behind a seemingly fragile exterior. All at once, he gathered the light around him, solidifying into an even more intense pattern. She could almost *see* it.

His human seeming was merely a guise. Dragon? Yes, she rather thought he might be. Dragons loved chocolate, and their eyes changed color just like that when they ate it.

She could feel the energy of him pinging against her skin, not painfully, but with authority. He was suddenly kind of loud, in the way storms are loud. The shadows gathered hints of storm in the corners of the room.

Holding the Rede of Trees within her body protected her from most beings, and her own nature was elusive enough to confuse the Others. Hiding in plain sight was a skill she appeared to share with her visitor. It was good that she had trained herself to be observant. Most people wouldn't even notice his eyes change color.

She grinned at him, prompting invitingly.

"So, Gran?"

He seemed taken aback that she was apparently amused by him.

"Why did you let me in?" he enquired. "I could be just anyone."

"Why are you avoiding the question?" she slung the conversation back to him.

"You are very confusing," he said, "not at all what I expected."

Visibly gathering his wits about him, he continued.

"Your Grandmother Argent and I were old friends." Mira was betting, to herself, that old meant just that, regardless of his apparent youth.

"We helped each other out from time to time, and she asked me to look in on you and help with the Book. We were due to meet when she unexpectedly," he paused, "left." He did rather seem put out. Changes of state could be hard on conversations.

"It took me a while to plan being in this world." He looked down and gestured at his body, a trifle embarrassed, "And then to get myself here."

"So there you were. Dragon." He looked startled that she had recognized him for what he was—a lucky guess.

"And you needed to find me?" she asked. He nodded.

"So what can you tell me about who was hunting Gran?" She sipped her own tea, now just cool enough for her to drink.

"She did not, perhaps, tell me it was a hunt." he said precisely. "She was too full of life to tell anyone her circumstances or plans. If I had to guess, it would be something to do with her assistant. Or perhaps even the Council. Her assistant was asking too many questions about the Rede, about whether it was safe. I know she was worried about it. It distracted her. In our business, you cannot afford distractions."

He was referring to the Council, Mira thought, and their habit of meddling with the affairs of Others. Gran had been a reluctant member for at least a few hundred years just to protect her own interests. She was what passed for being the responsible one in Mira's extended family. If rumor were true, Gran had something to do with founding the Council, which seemed a little far-fetched to Mira, given how acerbic Gran had been in talking about the Council's antics. Still, you never knew with Gran. She'd been around since the beginning of time and had been meddling with the affairs of Others for most of that time.

3

WISHBORN

It must have taken some degree of distraction for her grandmother to change state. Death was the word hereabouts; dead wasn't a word nearly complicated enough for beings like Gran. Beings like Gran measured their time in aeons. A little change of state might hardly be noticed from her point of view, much as it dismayed those who loved her. Mira had seen her Gran change forms as casually as most people changed clothing; no surprise then that Mira thought her absence was merely another change of shape.

Argent Astra had originally come into being as a star at the beginning of the universe. She had fallen into the world as a Wishborn, the only one of her kind in this World as far as Mira knew. A star who chooses to incarnate as an avatar, while some part lives on as a star, gets to keep her power Gran had said to her. Gran had been like that, if her bed time stories to a small Mira were anything to go by. Most of her power was concentrated into her current form.

Though Gran could apparently change form at will, shaping her wishes to different bodies over time, it was said the many forms of Others also came into being by wishing.

19

By the power of Gran's wishes more often than not. Even deities had been known to tremble before Gran's mischief. It had surprised everyone when she decided to leave the World of Form.

"She gave me this," he said, reaching into his shirt and drawing out a necklace on a silver chain. On it was a pendant Mira last seen when Gran had left the book with her. He pulled it off over his sable hair.

"For you, she said." Edward held it out to her.

It was a piece of the star stuff Gran had once been, and could not be taken, only given. Having it in his possession gave him Gran's seal of approval. It also made Mira's eyes mist up.

She missed Gran terribly, even though she knew she was somewhere 'out there', just not immediately available in the world.

As she took the gift from his hand, sparks flew, and the world seemed to tilt. She nearly dropped it. As it landed safely in her hand, it glowed for a moment, deep in the heart of the chunk of what looked like metal-fused-glass, she felt the warmth of her Gran's spirit for a long couple of heartbeats.

"Thank you" Mira whispered. "This means the world to me."

"So will you get the Rede and come with me?" he asked. "Justin, your Gran's assistant, cannot be far behind. He delayed me by asking questions, and I made a mistake. I thought he was honestly concerned when he asked all those questions about the Rede. I didn't answer him, but I may not have hidden where I was going well enough. I don't know if he will reach out to you, to find the answers to his questions."

Mira didn't know Justin but he sounded like someone to avoid, especially if a Dragon was wary of him. Not that a Dragon was exactly benign. This one was certainly anything but harmless, despite his current form. Mira wondered in passing where the rest of his Dragon was resting, while he was here, compressed into being a rather small human. She could ask, however one danger at a time seemed prudent. Being around him at all was surely enough.

"Where do you want us to go?" She thought of the phone calls and favors she would need to call in to keep the public library open. People must be able to borrow books; that was the important thing. But organizing that could wait.

"I need to fetch something first," Mira said aloud. Grabbing her keys, she opened the filing cabinet and pulled out an oversized tapestry messenger bag. She started stuffing candy bars, water bottles and a tea-infuser into it.

Moving over to the book trolley, she grabbed a leather book from the drawer in the center. She unplugged her phone from the wall charger where she left it most days. She thought ahead to what she would need for an indefinite time. "We'll need to go to my apartment first," she said.

"Somewhere safe," he said, answering Mira's question. That likely meant somewhere defensible, she thought. Dragons tended to think that way. Mira recalled that they also became impatient.

"Go get your jacket" she said. "I'll get a couple of things and join you back at the door."

She needed to get him out of the way so she could fetch a couple of rare books from the stacks. Those books were not as important as Gran's book, but chronons were bound up in them. They were her responsibility and her joy, but they were not exactly safe. It would not be fair to leave them in the library without her being around to mediate who got to read them.

4

HOME AND AWAY

She indicated with a gesture that he should drive as she folded her athletic body into the passenger seat of a BMW convertible. She was both surprised and relieved that they would travel by normal means. While he could likely transport her, his true form was way too massive for her to try to transport him.

The car however, only needed to deal with his human form and weight in this world. He managed to bang his knee as he got behind the wheel, which made her smile again, but once there he settled into being one with the car.

The drive uptown to the apartment was short but hectic. She wasn't sure why he drove his BMW better than his new body, although he did seem to think speed limits were for other people.

Once she was sure he could manage, she gave him directions to her apartment in the University District. It wasn't far, even at this busy time of day.

Meanwhile she focused on calls to set up arrangements with Abby and Adam, chums from college, to cover her unexpected absence at the Suzzalo extension library.

She had left her car keys for Abby, along with a note in the library desk. Abby would keep an eye on Dr. Horrible, her mixed Persian cat.

"Okay, that's arranged" Mira said, ringing off from Adam just as they parked on the street. Adam was pretty flexible about taking extra shifts when she took vacation.

She'd told him this was sudden family business.

"How much time do we have?" she asked Edward.

"Can we be out of here in an hour?" he answered hopefully, with an air of wistfulness. Clearly he was not accustomed to people who moved expeditiously.

"Sure," she said. "Are cats a problem for you?" Mira was looking forward to seeing what Dr. Horrible made of the Dragon, and vice versa.

A few minutes later she got to see Dr. Horrible sniff the intruder's extended fingers, hunch his back and fluff out his fur as if to start something. Then he disdainfully stretched and yawned, settling back into fake kitty slumber. Mira was not fooled. He was going to pointedly ignore the stranger.

The Dragon wrinkled his nose and straitened his jacket while adjusting his glasses, which she guessed said much the same thing. Mira saw they were going to be aloof about it, which was a shame. She'd been kind of looking forward to twenty pounds of chocolate Persian cat versus the Dragon.

"Make yourself at home." She gestured at the living room, "Kitchen is through the arch."

She decided to let him assume the Rede was one of the books she'd grabbed from the library. It would save explanations, as well as give her more time to assess what he was really about.

Why was he here now, rather than a few years ago when Gran passed? Mira had heard that *Others* had an odd sense of time, but that did not balance with his sudden appearance in a terrible hurry.

She picked up the go-bag backpack she kept ready, a habit that Gran had instilled in her when she was a small child. Mira quickly added useful things into corners, as well as another pair of rolled up socks with some favorite, though inexpensive, jewelry stuffed safely inside. Her messenger bag held all the important things, so this bag was just for insurance really. It did not seem she would be back quickly, so her favorite colorful jewelry would be a comfort. The important jewelry, the magical charms, she would wear.

A quick shower later, she was dressed to go, well within twenty minutes. She replaced the stick in her hair with a more substantial hair clasp, tucked a tinted chap stick into her pocket, and called her appearance presentable.

Sweeping up a couple of talismans, including one to help her be safer or at least more fireproof, along with a handful of ward stones. She placed the talismans over her head, then under the layers of shirt and a light comfortable sweater. She stuffed a heavier jacket into her pack in case she needed it. It was quilted silk, so it compacted down well. Mira pushed a knife in a scabbard down into her scuffed boot to supplement the folding blade in her pocket. Adjusting the straps of the backpack, she slung her shoulder bag across her chest, taking a couple of deep breaths, and settled her Chi. The backpack settled easily; she did a lot of hiking on weekends so it didn't even feel heavy.

As she came back into the living room, she heard knocking on the neighboring apartment door. Sound traveled in these older places. It was a good thing for her that she and her neighbor has switched apartment numbers. It stopped both of them from being annoyed by the wrong callers. Friends always seemed to know which apartment was the right place when they came to visit. Maybe the 'Touch not the cat!' sign was their hint. Messing with Dr. Horrible would likely be trouble for anyone who tried such a foolish thing.

As she noticed the disturbance, the Dragon whirled towards the sound outside the door. He seemed to be impatient and irritated, in a way that concerned her. An irritated beast was a danger best avoided. He moved purposefully towards her, reaching for her in a single flickering movement. She just had time to hear the sound of Dr. Horrible yowling at the unexpected energy as the world went away.

Caught up in his arms, adrift in the wave that was a Dragon-in-motion, they were all at once elsewhere. The light fractured into a chiaroscuro of light and shadow. She fragmented into a million dancing prisms in an empty place. There was a pressure that was not movement, slipping between moments. Time became compressed, creating intense sensation, spiking as the chronons resonated within her. She screamed, splintered, coalesced, and every living shadow went dark.

5

AWAKENING

Coming back took a long time. Mira whimpered as pain blanketed her senses. Waves of color and memory unfolded within her, until finally she woke. When she opened her eyes, it looked like light was bleeding from every surface. Wherever here was, the Dragon was in trouble when she got her hands on him.

It felt a bit like having migraine. Colors were shifted, light seemed more intense, and it hurt. A lot. Yet, as she carefully stood up, grabbing her pack and shoulder bag, she noticed that her balance and center were also off, and that didn't happen with migraine. They weren't off by much, yet to someone who always knew exactly where she was in space and time, that little change was alarming. Something in the transition had shifted things inside her. Or maybe it was some interaction between the Rede and the shift in place and time. It would take some meditation and energy work to scope out the edges of the shift. But now was the time to go find, and perhaps confront, the Dragon.

Doors across the room beckoned. Large heavy doors of metal over wood, though they appeared to be counterbalanced, as they opened easily enough. She had been put to bed with a soft quilt over her and was still dressed in yesterday's clothes.

The hallway outside the room stretched in both directions. She chose left, which led to an atrium, with even more blinding light, and a wooden staircase. Sunshine continued to bombard her eyes as she moved down the stairs. The atrium appeared to span both levels, with a high vaulted ceiling, lots of wooden beams, and floor to ceiling windows that had her vision smearing. First thing, find a kitchen and have some tea, with big pain killers, and then she'd be in a better place to deal with wherever she had landed.

On the way through the ground floor, she noticed the furnishings were eclectic, tasteful, and in the style of 'Northwest ignorable'. Clearly not the Dragon's main residence. Unless he favored interior decorators and the color bland, this was not his place.

When she located the kitchen, behind the blond sandstone central fireplace, she headed for the stove and turned on the kettle. She appropriated a mug hanging under the cupboard, ignored the coffee pot entirely, and rummaged in her bag for some decent Oolong tea and her infuser. Swallowing a couple of aspirin with some water, she closed her eyes and waited for the kettle to be ready.

"There you are" said Edward. "I hope you don't mind that I put you upstairs." He was back to hesitant mode, which made it much harder to yell at him for the abrupt translocation.

Sighing, she pushed away from the cupboard.

"Dragon. Edward," she said, pulling herself up to her full five feet eight inches and a half. "Where are we?"

"A friend's house in the San Juan islands" he replied. "I thought we could stop here and make plans."

"And the problem with my place was?"

"Ah. I may have moved too quickly." He sounded apologetic. "There was someone near your door. I heard knocking and it felt like Justin was getting too close."

"Hmm. Well, next time, ask me before shifting me, okay?" There, that sounded somewhat reasonable, though she felt anything but reasonable about the lingering effects of the shift. There was no sense yelling until she had more information. At his nod, she continued.

"Tell me about Justin then?" she invited, finishing up her tea and moving to the kitchen table to curl up in a nearby chair next to her bags, just in case he made a move towards being away again. She wasn't exactly trusting him.

"Do you know him?" he asked.

"No," she replied. "He was a relatively new addition, I think. Gran mentioned a research assistant a few years back, before she went away, but he didn't occupy much of our conversation. I never met him."

"He was studying with her. Some of the old knowledge. Arcana. Sigils. Helping her with archiving some research she was pursuing for the Council. He became a bit of a personal secretary." He paused, clearly thinking about what to say next. "Since your Gran went away, he's been organizing her papers and her Collections. He started carefully asking one or two of her friends about the Rede of Trees. Argent must have had some mention of it in her notes."

"He didn't know I had it then?" she asked.

"No. I don't think he suspected you knew anything about it until I made a mistake, and mentioned that I was going to come and see you, on an errand from your Gran."

"Good." Mira stated firmly. "Then let us keep it that way." She thought rapidly. "Any chance you can let him think the errand is a simple message or delivery of a sentimental, but unimportant, keepsake? You did bring the pendant," she ventured, "so it would fit."

"My transition has made me less careful than usual," he admitted. "Yet he is unlikely to think any keepsake from Argent is unimportant." He paused, looking meaningfully at the pendant around her neck. "I do not want to chance meeting with him, and revealing anything at all to him at this point in time."

"Drat." I said with some feeling. "Okay, then, what did Gran tell you about the Rede?"

"We talked about it over many years. She said it was knowledge from the Forever Forest, encoded on the inner bark of ancient trees. She said that it was magically instilled into a hidden Library. Baphomet was said to be one of the keepers, or custodians, and had passed it along to her. Argent said," Edward added quietly, "that she had added her own experience from speaking with trees to it, as well as the Star Scrolls. That means it contains some of the oldest knowledge in all the Worlds." He paused, searching her face for understanding.

"Okay, I get it. Big important magic." She wondered what Gran had been thinking when she left the Rede with Mira. Dangerous knowledge that everyone searching for Power would be desperate to control. Just great. It was a good thing she had been practicing the Quiet Way to keep her power-hungry family from paying attention to her movements.

"What did she tell you she wanted you to do, Edward?" Mira asked.

"Protect you. Help you with the Rede," he said seriously. "She said you were the new custodian."

"Damn!" Mira said with feeling. "Gran implied it was temporary. That I was just going to hold it for her for a while. Clearly we have a different idea of what 'a while' means." She was suddenly furious. With Gran. With the Dragon. With how this had landed in her lap after all her efforts to walk away from the past, her family, the dangerous heritage she'd always feared would catch up with her.

Her father's side of the family was complicated. And their machinations for power, for control, were so ingrained in them that it made her crazy. They never had understood her pleasure in quiet contemplation, let alone the treasure she found in cultivating good friendships. She'd made herself a distant and infrequent visitor home for more than one reason and now she was back in the thick of it. Like it or not.

Fuel for thought.

First things first, though. Breakfast. There would be no clear planning without some calories, with a resulting rise in blood sugar, on board.

6

BREAKING FAST

D o you mind if I rummage in the kitchen and make breakfast?" she aimed the question at the Dragon. Getting up, she moved in the direction of the kitchen.

"You cook? Human food?" the yearning in his voice was quite clear.

"What have you been feeding yourself?" she asked, briskly heading for an oversized refrigerator. Eggs, cheese, onions, mushrooms, peppers, fresh garlic. Glancing around, she grabbed a cast iron skillet, intercepting his momentary look of alarm with a grin. No, she didn't have any issues with cold iron; she was grateful for that. A couple of her uncles broke out in hives at the mere sight of it.

"Urmmm" he hesitated. "Sunlight?" he ventured, his voice rising in question. "It seems to be usable but it is not very tasty in this form." He looked down at his lanky human body.

Startled at his reply, she laughed out loud.

"Let's fix that shall we?" she said, chopping ingredients with a chef-quality knife. His host, the owner of the bland décor, was obviously much better acquainted with what made a good kitchen. Everything just where she would expect it to be. Either the owner of the place cooked a lot, or was watching *Iron Chef* and the Cooking Channel rather more often than Mira managed herself. The routine tasks of making food relaxed her. She found some of the headache starting to recede.

Sweating the onions in butter and olive oil while she chopped the fresh garlic and parsley, mushrooms and peppers, Mira quickly started to prepare small dishes of diced vegetables. The technique of preparing the small dishes of ingredients before assembling the elements into a recipe was second-nature to her.

The smell made her mouth water; onions in butter were a weakness she was not interested in overcoming. Within a few minutes, she sautéed the ingredients and whisked the eggs with some garam masala, a complex Indian spice that she liked for the mellow, warming flavor. She poured the whipped eggs over the sautéed vegies and used a spatula to ensure everything cooked evenly.

Stirring the food with intent, she absently added a charm of good digestion and easy communication. One large omelet, halved, and then cut in two, made generous portions on the plates. She made quick toast from a thick cut loaf of bread and transferred the plates back to the table. Together with orange juice and another cup of tea, life was looking much more manageable.

While she could, and did, eat almost everything, including leftovers and granola bars when she had to, Mira preferred to make good food whenever possible. It gave the body strength, and the spirit energy.

Whole foods were so much better than the mystery food her friends ate so often. She also had the notion that she may get the Dragon to be even more forthcoming if she fed him. Hungry Dragons could be so unpredictable, and she was not looking forward to being an accidental meal.

The next little while was occupied by enthusiastic consumption, interrupted by the occasional sounds of pleasure all beings make when enjoying a good meal. His manners appeared to improve by the moment as he copied her movements.

She had the odd sense that his body was even newer than she had first surmised. His attempt at eating sunlight to fuel his human body seemed evidence enough of that. Others always seemed to think they could power a human form the same way they'd treat a construct; it always took them a while to work out that creating another true form, whatever that form was, meant that they had to feed it the correct kind of fuel or food for that form.

At least he hadn't passed out like her cousin Daniel did when he first tried creating a new form. She had teased Daniel about that for so years, she still got a laugh from it. Sitting back at length, she sipped her tea, gazing at him over the rim.

"Anything else you can tell me about Justin or his interest in the Rede?" she asked.

"I tolerated him well enough, whenever I saw him," he offered, "though he did not interest me. Human. Male. Annoying habit of lurking about in corners and trying to listen to conversations not meant for him. I could never see why Argent bothered with him."

Mira had a few ideas about that. Gran had a habit of playing with her food. If he was attractive and useful, Gran may have found more to recommend him than a Dragon would notice or care about. Something for Mira to consider.

A student or assistant of Gran would pick up all kinds of interesting information, and if Justin was an occasional bed-mate as well, he may have some ideas about his entitlement to Gran's knowledge when she disappeared. Mira hoped that was all it was. Though power could be shiny and enticing, pursuit of it rarely turned out the way people expected.

"Human. That could be interesting," she said aloud.

"They leave so quickly. Not enough time to learn their own names, let alone create a story. And they're crunchy," he ended apologetically. "They always seem to want to talk to you. And when I used to eat them, they would get stuck in my teeth."

Mira pointed to her chest. "Human..."

He laughed, shaking his finger from side to side in disagreement.

"Well, mostly human—on my mother's side of the family tree."

"Custodian of the Rede says otherwise," he returned. "And you don't, ahh, smell human."

Tilting her head to one side, she had to ask "what does human smell like?"

"Snack food."

She laughed. She could hardly complain if she didn't like the answer he gave her. Okay. Moving right along.

"So Justin was working as Gran's secretary," she said. "Making himself useful. Doing the usual. Trading for enough influence to get himself a longer life, or more options."

"Something like that," he agreed.

"Is there any reason to believe he had anything to do with her death?"

"I do not think so. There were too many who became interested in where Argent was getting her information from. Knowledge the Council members found inconvenient at best."

"Knowledge that they did not have access to?"

"Yes. I do not know the source, even though we sometimes worked together." He sounded aggrieved, and he was speaking truth. She had an instinct for truth.

"How long was her knowledge inconvenient, before she was tricked into leaving the world?" Mira asked.

"Tricked? How did you know about the duel?"

"Guessing." she admitted, which was, strictly speaking, true. "What are you hiding from me?" Obviously a lot, but Mira needed to stay on the offensive to get more information to shape a picture.

"She agreed to a word duel. The terms included the winner leaving their life, with the loser offering up a future promise. Argent won, so she was the one to leave the world. I think your Uncle was surprised that she chose to leave as she did, dissolving into light and fire."

"My uncle?" She had quite a few uncles, so it would be good to narrow things down a bit.

"Priam," he responded. "He was the one who challenged her."

"Did anyone else hear the terms?" she asked. It would help enormously, if there were witnesses.

"No-one was near enough to hear the duel. It was thought to be about a Council matter."

"Five years ago!" she said with some heat. "And only now do I find out my uncle was the one who caused her to depart?"

Damn. Only one of her benighted family would have a clue how to trick Gran out of pursuing a life in the World of Form. They must have had her give her word in just the right way. Gran was a stickler for the exact adherence to her word. But it didn't make sense. To be effective, Gran must have wished to leave. Only wishing would make it so.

"My apologies for the delay," he said sincerely. "This body took me a while."

"Apologies accepted," she said absently, observing the niceties. "But one of my wretched cousins might have mentioned it. They do use phones occasionally."

"They may not have known," he ventured. "Only the Council and a few independent observers were there."

"Okay. Back to the Council and their knowledge snit. How long was that going on?"

"Not long. Only for a decade or two. There were some changes. They were trying to control who got access to the Kasik, the Deep, and the Library, though your Gran stopped them cold on most fronts. Her Domain."

"As far as I know, they've always been trying to do that."

"Yes, but they were trying harder. And succeeding to some measure."

"Is that working with the Others?"

"Not so much. That is part of the Council's issue. Argent was always a force of her own. If anyone sought knowledge of the mysteries, those who walked those paths seemed to be drawn to her. It was almost like anyone Other found a thread of kinship with her."

"We're going to need to know more about that duel", said Mira decisively. "Who might know more? Apart from Justin, that is. I'd like to avoid him for a while."

"I hate to suggest it," suggested the Dragon, "but your Uncle Priam might be the only one who can help answer questions you might have about that."

"Dealing with my family is almost never a good idea," she stated, "and I want to think about it for a bit. How safe are we here? I'd like to go for a walk, and think about what you've told me."

"Safe enough. We are off the grid, and I don't own this house. My friend keeps this place to drop in on films being made in the area. There is only one other house on the island. Alyn says it is owned by another software guy. He only makes it up here in the summer, and that is almost over."

"See you later then." Mira grabbed her day bag and slung it across her chest to sit against her hips. Hands free, she gestured a question.

"There's a path down to the water from the deck." He pointed towards the French doors across the room.

7

FINDING CENTER

Mira let herself out into a particularly fine September day. There were some clouds on the horizon, yet the near sky was clear. The deck had more than a full wide view of Puget Sound. Steps led down to a path that wound its way through the moss-covered rocks and trees.

Fallen cedar and birch branches along the path gave silent evidence of yesterday's wind and rain. Storms often blew up quickly in the islands, and just as suddenly evaporated at this time of year. The day was shaping up to be hotter than usual. Mira reached into a pocket to pull out a couple of hair spikes to pull her hair up off her neck. Taking off her jacket, she tied the arms around her waist. Not fashionable, but she was comfortable with herself.

In appearance, she was just another Northwest nature girl. Flyaway, curly long dark blond hair, strong square face with a large mouth and slightly tilted larger-than-normal eyes from her mixed heritage. Her skin was a smooth even light tan, her body athletic, with long limbs and capable hands, nails short but tinted with metallic polish. She favored muted dark jewel colors and casual drapes to the fabrics. Her boots were black, low heeled and were scuffed old friends. She could walk all day in them over any terrain. She'd tested that last year on an archeological dig with her college friend, Ellis.

Reaching a natural lookout, a clearing with mostly large flat rocks jutting out over the water, she decided to stop for a while. It looked like the perfect place to breathe, watch the water, and allow the stress of the last day to recede.

For a while, she just watched the water. Sending her attention out, she varied her focus in the liminal places. Where the sky met the water, where the water met the rocks, and where the water met the tumbled rocks on the shore. In the in-between places, the balance kept shifting. It felt like a good match for the liminal shift that was happening inside her. She needed to reach some sense of calm again.

Mira was not sure how she felt about being responsible for the Rede. When she agreed to look after it for Gran, she had not asked enough questions. Not about what it was, nor how it may be to hold it over time. She'd really thought it would be a month or two. And Gran, to be fair, had told her she needed it kept safe. It had seemed so simple. Say yes to offering Gran a favor, balance out some of what she owed Gran for making a place for her and a home when things were odd with the family.

It wasn't a bad family exactly; she just wasn't like the rest of her mother's artistic clan, being more interested in research and books than in painting or dance. Her father's family was not exactly normal either, and considered martial arts, mayhem, and the pursuit of power to be preferred activities. Her mother had her adventurous phase when she hooked up with her father, though both of them seemed a little embarrassed by the whole affair.

Mum had a genius for ignoring things that she did not want to think about. Her life had moved on from romance with a magical being, and back into her Art and her studio. It would be easy to think of her whole relationship with Mira's father as a painting she once created, or a piece of performance art. Intensely present and then gone again. Except for Mira's subsequent existence of course.

Well, that was water well under the bridge. There was no point in dwelling on how she felt about both sides of her family. While they had their good points, she may as well be a changeling to each side. She sent those thoughts aside to drift away with the water on the shore.

Living with Gran had always been much more her cup of tea, enriched as it was with books, research, games and whimsy. Those games had a habit of being deadly earnest from time to time, as Gran had taught her more magic, dressed up as games, than most people got in a life-time of study.

More to the point, Gran loved her and encouraged her to explore whatever and wherever she liked. That training was to the chagrin of the Council, as Gran did not place any of the precious Council's knowledge beyond her reach. Beyond her grasp now, that was a different thing; if you could hold a dangerous thing, then you'd earned some right to it. Some things you need to learn in order, and that was the point of some of Gran's teaching.

But the Rede? Leaving it with her for this long was surely too dangerous, even for one of Gran's teaching games. The last two custodians, or keepers if you liked that term, had been a daemon or god, Baphomet, and her Gran, who was the living avatar of a star. So what did that mean for her?

The Rede appeared to have some unexpected qualities. It felt like the Rede's energy was blowing though her head like a changing wind, stirring up potential and magic in her that was new and strange. Though being the Rede, it was much more likely the energy it was stirring was eldritch and ancient. Mira wondered how that would express itself through her mixed heritage.

Mira had magic in abundance, though most of the time she used it to make life comfortable or to avoid being messed with, rather than to change the world. Unlike her cousins and uncles. They used magic to control and dominate. It had always rather pissed them off that their magic slid off her like water off a duck. Likely just as well, as she had a feeling the Rede had planted a great big 'eat me' sign over her head.

Too much musing though and not enough action, she thought. If she wanted a clearer hold on reality, she'd best take this time to center and anchor her energies, and to re-assert her kinesthetic sense of where she was in time and space. Some breathing, some qiqong exercises, and meditation would be a good start, and this was a good place, between the water and the sky.

8

FREEING THE BODY

Mira decided to take off her boots, jacket, and bag, to give herself freedom to move. Starting with a set of exercises to free the body, she began with head and neck relaxation. Running her hands through her hair, she loosened the tension in her scalp and face, before moving on to massage the back of her neck with both hands. She followed that up with shoulder rolls in each direction. Lifting, rotating, and letting go after rolling her shoulders from front to back, and then the same in reverse. Next she focused on opening her chest and back, where so much tension seemed to have taken up residence. It surprised her how tense she had become.

Folding her arms at chest height, fists closed, with thumb tucked in, back of hands upward, fists just touching, she took a deep breath and rotated her elbows backward. She pulled back until she could feel the muscles in her back bunch. She added some spring in the movement, compressing and releasing the muscles, breathing deeply for the count of three, and then rest. Do it again and again, until the shoulder-blades let go. Finally.

Opening her right fist to cup the other, she pressed her fist into her palm, feeling the chest muscles jump. Three times, and then change palms, pressing now into her left palm. Finish by bowing her head slightly, breathing deeply and evenly. Already she could feel a sense of release.

Next, those pesky hips needed some work. Bending her knees slightly, and centering her weight, she imagined a line running down through the center of her body, through the energy centers that blossomed deep inside her, down deep into the earth. The imaginary line extended up through her head towards the center of a star.

Leaving her arms loose, she turned from side to side, allowing the arms to loosely wrap around her body. The easy swivel movements from side to side loosened up her hips and lower back. Next, she placed her hands with palms flat against her lower back, just below her waist. With legs straight now, she leaned left, forward, right and back, moving her weight from leg to leg, rotating her hips all the way around in one direction, before reversing and rotating in the other direction.

Moving downwards, she placed her feet together, and bent her knees forward, making a dipping motion to the right three times, and then to the left. She could feel her right knee pop a little, releasing as she moved. Then it was time for the ankles. Raising up on her toes she stretched the arches. Then she rocked back on her heels three times, and repeated toes, heels, toes and heel rocks. When she was done with the physical releases, she was feeling much more present in her body.

Next, she would move breath with her energy, what she had learned from a Chinese teacher to call her Chi. It had surprised her that breath work with her Chi was intended to bring chaos into the body with the breath, rather than calm. Master Chen said that energy tends to pool in the body, to become stagnant. That by using active breath, chaos entered in, acting on the stagnant energy, breaking it up with chaos. When the energy was again moving without becoming still, the body would return to balance, and healthy flow would be restored.

She took the first stance, feet at shoulder width apart, knees bent, hands loosely cupped with palms facing forward. She placed her tongue just behind her teeth, and breathed in through her nose, and out through her mouth. This completed a circuit of energy in the body that would otherwise be open and passive. The tongue behind her teeth made the breathing cycle active and generative, so more energy would enter in with each breath.

She raised her arms and moved her hands to just in front of her chest, cupped, imagining a ball of light and energy between them. She could see the ball form with the Sight. Pushing the ball away from her body, directly out at chest height, she breathed out. Breathing in, she pulled the ball back towards the body, feeling the energy move between her hands. Her body, breath and energy were flowing in a smooth movement. She repeated this movement five times, once for each element.

For the next step, she rolled the ball upwards, along with her hands, until her hands were over her head, and she was looking at the ball of energy over her head as she breathed out. Breathing inwards, she rolled it down again until it rested at her solar plexus center. Then back upward, breathing out, to the energy center on the top of her head, her crown.

For the first couple of cycles, she felt the energy on the outside of her subtle body. After the first two times, however, her resistance faded, the energy ball expanding until it was rolling through her energy centers, massaging and loosening up knots as it went. Rolling up through her heart, throat, her third eye, and up to the crown as she breathed out, and back down again to the heart and solar center on the way down.

Time for the rest of the body. Coming to rest at the solar center in the middle of her chest, she could already feel her head clearing. Her headache was gone, and her breathing had deepened. The world felt more alive, and she could feel the connections between every living thing. The tangled confusion of the past day seemed to fade away like mist.

Rolling the energy ball downwards to her tan tien, just below her navel, and her hands with it, she repeated the pattern, rolling back up through her body to her solar plexus again. Repeating it five times, she finished up by pivoting on one heel to the right and rolled the ball down. Bending, she rolled it down to her foot, and back. First to the right, and then to the left.

Mira almost felt restored to herself. However, they would soon be moving again, so she took the time to work through a set of magical energy exercises, and her martial arts form as well. By the time she was finished, she was feeling loose, coordinated, and in the present moment. The time energies within her were also coming into balance again.

She quickly dressed again in socks, boots, jacket and bag, then walked down to the shore to pick up a token to remind her of this place, should she wish to return. Taking one last cleansing breath, Mira headed back up the path towards the house.

As she moved into the woods, a breeze picked up, bringing the scent of cedar, moss and resin with it. The dappled light was silvery between the majestic trees. Ferns and salmon berries grew along the path, along with wild mushrooms and grasses that looked like they'd escaped their landscaped borders.

The chronons that flirted with her own energy seemed much more coherent now. The possibilities were braided, and clearer. She could see where to place her feet on the path.

9

PLANNING

As she arrived back at the house, the sky was clouding over, in a fairly typical Northwest region weather change. Her friends joked that while other places had climate Seattle had weather, lots of it. She had learned to layer clothing just like the Seattle folks did. It may not be the height of fashion, but it appealed to her practical side.

"I'm back," she called out, slipping through the French doors.

"Did you have a good walk?" Edward asked.

"It was great. I'm going to head for a shower. Will we have time for me to throw my clothes through some laundry?"

"That will be—ah, I don't know about where?" He said, looking a bit mystified about the prospect of laundry.

"Don't worry about it. I can find the laundry, if we have time." Pausing at the table to grab fresh clothes from her bag, she asked "Will we be staying here today and tonight, so we can make plans?"

"I thought so?"

"Great. Then I'll see you shortly." Heading for the stairs, she paused and turned again. "Can you think about who we might ask about Gran's duel? Maybe we could go visit them tomorrow?"

As she bounced up the stairs she thought how odd it must be for him, out in the world in a new body. Of course, his other form, the Dragon, was still present, and showed through now and then. That couldn't be what was making him so diffident though, she mused. I mean, hello Dragon! Ancient being who'd obviously known Gran for a long time, she thought to herself wryly. It was kind of sweet of him to conjure up a body just to come see her. He was obviously uncomfortable, so she guessed that he hadn't seen much reason to change forms before this. Either that, or his manner was due to something else entirely. It made her wonder what else was going on. What could be making an Other feel so uncertain?

10

MOMENTS IN TIME

The shower only took a few minutes. Mira supposed she could have stretched it out, but she had the notion that she'd tested Edward's patience a little already. The bathroom had been a bit of a welcome surprise. It was much more luxurious, and varied from the bland décor in the rest of the house. The walk-in shower had deep green tile, and the walls were a rich, deep chocolate. She had made good, if quick, use of the spa products and the moisturizer left out for guests. The shower had great water pressure, too.

Having fresh socks and underwear, clean from the skin out, felt great. Mira had six pairs of socks tucked into various corners of her bag, and likely just as many knickers. She changed into her favorite pomegranate colored tank top, pulled on a tunic that was deep purple, and called it good. The Dragon wouldn't care what she looked like, but the vibrant colors matched her new mood. Colors to match her aura was likely going a bit far, yet it was a harmless indulgence.

The laundry was just where she had expected it to be, downstairs behind the staircase. While Mira didn't much like doing laundry, or dishes for that matter, that all changed when traveling. You took advantage of what pit stops you could get, and took care of practical things. It gave travelers a rest from each other, and gave you something to do with your hands while thinking.

"The kettle just boiled," he said unexpectedly as she arrived back at the living room.

Making tea was a universal in her world. It was one of the few things both sides of her odd family agreed on. It didn't matter what the circumstances were, if there was a conversation to be had, they would put on the kettle and make a nice cup of tea. He must have noticed that her go-to action was making tea.

"I have been thinking about who we might ask about the duel," he ventured, as they sat down with cups at the table.

"Do you happen to remember Jin Rael, from the Council?"

"Yes, he was there when I was growing up", she said excitedly. "I remember him being interested in me and he didn't need to be. We spent a lot of time playing odd games. He always asked after my dreams, as if they were important somehow."

"He is someone who I think well of," he said thoughtfully, "and was an ally to Argent on more than one occasion. Perhaps even a friend."

"I remember Gran saying that they were friends," she said, "and he often stopped by for afternoon tea. He was surprisingly friendly to a small girl who asked too many questions." Mira remembered him with some fondness. He had even been her magical mentor for a while when she was a kid. The Djinn was a stickler for proper forms of protocol, and had helped her learn the basics. Yet he was thoughtful of her feelings, and seemed to treat children with more latitude than he offered most of the people who came into his princely presence.

"Do you think he might be willing to talk to us?" Mira asked.

"I think it may be possible", he paused, "though we may need to travel to him, and he is somewhere called The Blue Mountains outside of Sydney, in Australia.

"Have you been there before?" she asked. She wasn't looking forward to another transition, but going to the other side of the world, and getting quick answers, did not seem to warrant her making a fuss about the method of transportation. A plane ride would take over a day and that did not seem convenient.

She wondered if a Dragon would even be willing to take commercial aircraft. Maybe as a bet, or as part of an elaborate game of some kind. The mental image she had was of stuffing something with a larger magical potential than any plane into the small seat afforded in the belly of a regular commercial aircraft. Her mental cartoon balloon was beyond absurd.

"I was there just ten years ago," he affirmed. "I have a good location for where we visited, near Norman's Pool at the Lindsay Gallery. We could contact him and see if it might be convenient to visit tomorrow."

"That would be good" she agreed. "I recall that he does not like to be disturbed at home without some notice. At least, that's what Gran said. I always saw him at Gran's Library."

"I will take care of discovering if a visit would be welcome, and then will return," he offered. He went off to some other room to make private contact with Jin Rael.

While he was gone, Mira rummaged in her bag to find notepaper and a drawing pen. If they were going to brainstorm a plan, it might help if she started with a list of what they knew, as well as the questions that were starting to pile up.

Her list began with "Rede. Custodian. Justin. Duel. Uncle Priam. Was Gran reachable? Check in with parents. Travel with the Dragon? Chronons. What internal changes are happening? What does the world have to bring to it? Tarot reading."

She could always add to it later. At least it was a beginning in organizing her thoughts. Mira felt better already just by writing things down. It seemed to get some of the new elements of her life into order, or at least out of her head.

11

INTO THE FRAY

After an afternoon and evening of planning, they had arrived at a few conclusions. They had even more questions though, and it appeared that the Dragon Edward, she reminded herself, was more impressed with the Rede than she had imagined an ancient lizard would be. Over the course of the evening, she had dodged several questions hinting that he would like to see it. However, she was not yet ready to admit she carried it within her. He still thought the Rede was an artifact, a physical book, one that she had with her in the capacious tote bag.

Are you ready, Mira?" Edward asked her.

"As ready as I'll ever be." She checked her backpack, settled her messenger bag, centered her energies, shielded, and only then reached out to take his hand, smiling a little.

This time the transition was not so bad. That may have had something to do with having advance notice. Or perhaps it was that she was deliberately shielding herself from the energies of the Dragon shift through space and time. She could feel the Rede more clearly this time. It was a little like she and the Rede were separate, yet some part of each shared a space. It seemed to her that it was in the liminal place where they overlapped that chronons shifted the possibilities into probabilities. Mira had the sense that a deeper part of her psyche, the part that worked intuitively with time energy, understood what that meant. However, that part of her communicated best through metaphor and dreams.

As they transitioned, she saw a blur of images, heard a cacophony of sounds, and smelled a dusty resinous scent. Then they were on the other side of the world, somewhere with a different quality of light. The sounds turned out to be hundreds of colorful birds, shrieking at their arrival. One of them sounded like it was laughing at them; other birds screeched, and in the distance something was making the sound of a rusty children's swing set. The dry, resinous scent was Eucalyptus Gum, and a rustling sound came from the long the dusty grasses around a natural-looking pool. A concrete life-sized statue of a woman peered sideways at them, a secret smile on her upturned lips. Across from her was an urn full of tiny orange and red orchids.

The place must be Norman's Pool, that fabled place where it was said all possibilities gathered, she realized. It was said to be a place where a traveler, were they to wait here, could meet anyone and everyone, real or imagined, including those who lived more properly in stories. The latter seemed a little far-fetched, though given her life of late, she was hardly in a place to question the power of fables and stories. For all she knew, the characters of fiction could gather enough belief to manifest in the world, much like some of the heroes who had become deities in earlier times.

They had arrived in the Blue Mountains, near the town of Faulconbridge. Australia had the opposite season from the United States, being on the other side of the equator, though it was around the same temperature now as a late Seattle summer. Here, the weather was just starting to warm up. If today's temperature was anything to judge by, in the high seventies, in not-quite spring, then the summer must be like a sauna.

The resinous foliage had a hint of greenish gray to it. Sharp scents and sweet mingled together, creating a heady but delicate bouquet of aromatic delight. The trees were also quite different, bearing intricate seed pods, varied shades of white and grey bark and sharply defined leaves. It was a place that encouraged a visitor to linger and enjoy their surroundings. It was a pity they had so much to accomplish today. She wistfully thought that it would be a good place to come back to. Mira carefully memorized some reference points, as well as noting the resonance of the emergence spot. By keeping the feeling of the place firmly in mind, she would be able to travel back here on her own.

Mira also found it helpful to take a token from places she wanted to travel to. It gave her a better connection to the place. Though Gran would say it was a crutch, Mira didn't see the harm in it. She would look around for a likely stone or seed pod to use as a travel token if time permitted. She was a little rusty with her travel magic, not having used it for a while. Travel by Dragon may be a little disconcerting, yet it was certainly quick and direct. Must thank Edward for the smooth transition she reminded herself.

12

NORMAN'S POOL

s Jin Rael meeting us here?"

"Yes, there's a nice tea shop." He smiled at her, and said, teasingly "It seemed auspicious."

She grinned back at him, willing to be teased a little about her love of the tea deva.

"Indeed."

"We are meeting him at the three maidens" which is, I think a test for us. "There is a path up that way." He gestured. "Let's see where it takes us".

They walked up some crumbling sandstone steps, past a couple of guardians wrought from the same concrete, a female satyr and cat woman or sphinx respectively, gazing at each other on opposite sides of the path. Mira was impressed by the artistry of the pair, and stopped to take a closer look. The figures were life-sized, and looked as if they had been modeled from life.

"The artist is, or rather was, Norman Lindsay," Edward said. "He worked in paint, stone, concrete, or just about anything he could get his hands on. This is where he lived and worked. The Gallery up ahead was where he lived a rather original bohemian life."

"The statues, they are almost alive," she mused. "Was he a magician then?"

"Not officially," he replied. "Though if the artist is good enough, formal training in the magical arts is not really necessary. His talent was deep enough that he drew on the Hidden Paths in his work."

They saw the start of a gravel path, with well-kept grass on either side up ahead. Following it to the right, it curved around and arrived at a large twisted tree. In front of the tree was another statue. This time, it was of three naked maidens, unabashedly fondling each other. A couple of teenage girls were pointing at it and giggling behind their hands, glancing over their shoulder at their conservative-looking parents, before running off towards the building alongside the tree. It seemed they wanted to see as much as they could before they were hauled off somewhere boring. This place must be quite a shock for parental sensibilities, Mira thought, with all the naked statues visible around the grounds. She was pleased to see the giggling girls though; the teenagers seemed to be enjoying their parents' discomfort.

When she glanced back at the three maidens, Jin Rael, an afreet, being another name for a djinn, stepped around the tree.

He was resplendent in a brocaded long vest, scarf, and jewelry. His long woolen trousers were tucked, absurdly, into what looked a bit like pirate boots. His long black hair shimmered with peacock highlights in the sunlight. He was wrapped in an illusion that gave his more fantastical features and impossible anatomy a human wrapper. Light bent around him in subtle ways, drawing attention only to the clothing, bending the attention away from looking too closely. Most people would only see a rather loudly baroque form, and not look closer.

"Princess! You are here," he exclaimed, reaching out dramatically to claim both her hands. "So strong you are and," he tilted his head to one side, "something is shimmering, in a rainbow, glimmering..."

"What have you done with my baby girl, Dragon?" he turned to Edward accusingly. "She is pretending to be all grown up." Muttering to himself, he abandoned her hands and stalked around her, sniffing the air. "You smell strange." Another sniff as he waved his hands, pulling shapes out of the air. "You smell of stardust and secrets." Throwing up his hands, he came to rest in front of the statue of the three maidens.

"Lovely to see you too," she said wryly.

"Tea!" he exclaimed, with an abrupt change of subject. "I am dying of thirst." He started walking backwards down the path, not paying a bit of attention to his feet, but nonetheless staying in the center of the path as it wound around the house.

"Where have you been lovely lady?" he asked. "What have you been dreaming?"

"You always ask me about my dreams." she commented. "But you never believe me."

"It hasn't happened yet," he stated, but then he stopped on the path, causing them to stop also to avoid colliding with him. She noticed Edward glancing between them, keeping his thoughts to himself. "Or has it? Hmmm?" He peered at her intently. "You will tell me?" he asked plaintively.

"I don't know what you mean." Though she did know, at least in part.

"Silly girl. Of course you do." He turned around and strode down the path. "Hurry up. The tea is waiting."

The Dragon wrapped himself in silence as they moved along, seemingly content to watch and listen attentively.

They passed a water tank up on stilts and some more trees and outbuildings. Over the ridge behind the house was a small building that contained the tea shop. The bushes alongside the path had prickly flowers, small seed pods and spiky looking foliage, most of them smelled interesting and spicy. Mira wished they had time to pause and examine the small flowers more closely.

13

BUSHMAN'S TEA

They ordered tea and scones at the counter of the tiny shop. Their footsteps echoed on the wooden floors as they made their way to a plain wooden table and practical plain chairs.

Surrounding them were families with children, an older couple over in the corner, and another set of laughing teenagers, boys this time. The bustle of chairs scraping on the floor, people arriving and leaving through the squeaking screen door, as well as the various laughter and excited voices made the tea shop much louder than she was expecting. It was busy, rather than private, and an odd choice, she thought, for their conversation.

The small meal, when it arrived on plain white plates, however, was delicious. The tea was dark and stout, a Bushman's tea the signs said, served with milk and sugar cubes on the side. The scones were more like flaky biscuits, rich with butter, served with rich strawberry jam and thick fresh cream.

"What trouble brings you here?" Jin Rael addressed the Dragon.

"Not trouble so much, good sir." Edward responded. "Rather, a search for more context."

"Ah. Just so." He nodded. "And you thought to ask me, a humble observer of events, for this clarity?"

"Indeed."

"Say on. Do." He steepled his fingers together under his chin, tilting his head to one side as he waited.

Edward glanced at Mira, silently asking if he should proceed. They just as silently agreed that he would give her precedence.

"Dearest Jin," she began. "I have come to ask for your help in easing my mind about Gran."

Jin looked thoughtfully at the Dragon, noting that he had ceded the question to her.

"What is it you wish to learn?" he responded carefully, redirecting the question.

"I wondered" she asked softly "if you had spoken to Gran before her duel with Uncle Priam?"

"Are you sure you want me to answer that here?" he enquired, glancing briefly at Edward.

"Please," she pleaded. "I would very much like to hear anything you feel you can say." There, she hoped she had said the right things to free him from obligation, and give permission for sharing things in front of Edward. She hoped that was not a mistake, though Edward had dealt honestly with her so far.

"Very well. Argent asked me to convey a message," he frowned, "but only if you asked." He waited with patience, saying nothing else. Mira realized that this was one of those occasions where she would have to follow the forms in order to learn more. And more, those forms must follow the pattern that both Gran and Jin Rael had drilled her in as a child.

"If it would please you, kind sir, I request and formally ask that you convey to me, here in this place, the message that the Star Born, known as Argent Astra, left in your keeping." She bowed formally, as part of the required steps of the dance.

The message she received was cryptic, phrased in a way that only made sense to her in context of her childhood with Gran. It reminded her of a game that Gran played with her as a child, and also of a token that she would need to pick up from her mother's house.

Mira was reminded that Jin Rael, as an afreet, dealt in wishes much as did Gran though in different ways. He was too powerful a being to have as an enemy, though a Djinn is also an unlikely friend, and can only be one when there is no obligation. He still seemed to want to be Mira's friend.

Or at least he wanted to stay close to find out what happened next in her dreams.

He had shared a foreseeing with her, without her even asking. His foreseeing showed her collecting interesting abilities, and he saw those abilities being triggered through dreaming. It could be that dream is a metaphor for the way in which the Rede seemed to be communicating with her by rummaging around in her head to find concepts, and to speak through her inner self in the language of dreams. At least, that was Mira's feeling at the moment. Time would tell if experience would write a different story.

14

DEPARTURES AND ARRIVALS

After tea and conversation, they headed back to Norman's Pool to leave before anyone else found them. Unfortunately, that was not to be. They reached the pool just as her Uncle Priam unexpectedly appeared out of the between. It was always interesting to see if you were looking right at the place of emergence, though mist seemed to hang close to the ground in most such places. Something about the emergence place made it difficult to focus on directly and most folks would find their eyes wandering past the spot without stopping on it. A bit of magical slight-of-hand Others had been relying on for aeons. Most people would see nothing out of the ordinary. For those who were sensitive in some way, they would argue away anything odd as merely imagination.

There was an impression of mist, but something more solid than mist. The between had no color of its own, though some echoes of the origin place would color the mist for a moment while the places were connected. The mist receded, revealing the traveler as if they had always been standing right there.

Her Uncle Priam has been knocking around the world for a long time. From some things he expressly did not say or confirm when the subject came up at a family dinner, Mira thought he may have been around for the events at Troy. She had even entertained the notion that he might actually be that Priam, or that stories after the fact confused him with that famous character.

Mira and her uncle had always had a tense relationship. Everyone expected they would get on famously on the face of it. They had both lived with Gran as young mages, though in his case, that was some millennia ago. Being a friendly child, she had been willing to be on good terms. However, he pretended a lot and expected her not to notice. His discounting her as a child, she could understand. Underestimating her intelligence? That annoyed her. Worse still, he pretended he liked her, when he did not. Priam gave the illusion of charm and affected a confident manner, when inside she could see he was full of insecurities. Perhaps the tension was envy or jealousy on his part, and yes, perhaps on her side as well. She could at least admit to that.

Both of them wanted to feel that they were Gran's favorite. Mira felt that he'd had his turn though, as he'd been Gran's ward and then her companion for many human lifetimes, and Mira had only had Gran for some twenty years. Drat the man. He made her doubt herself, and always had. She had a feeling it was mutual.

"Hello Uncle." She nodded respectfully, acknowledging their familial connection. There was no point in antagonizing him, and she may need to flatter him into being chatty. The necessity made her stomach hurt.

"Mira." He nodded carefully back, using her name, but not calling her 'niece'.

"Lord Eleison," he saluted the Dragon. "You have been much missed in chambers this last season." He paused. "I do hope your Hoard is to your liking ..." The latter comment was a polite, if insincere, attempt to observe the forms.

Mira waited for the expected greetings between her Uncle Priam and Jin Rael in vain. As she turned her head to where the afreet had been only moments before, there was a distinct lack of his energy, let alone physical form. He really was quite deft at disappearances, she thought. Something she could stand to learn from him.

"Thank you for your good wishes, Lord Priam." Edward nodded. "And your endeavors proceed well?"

"Well enough, thank you."

"Mira dear," Priam said, "are you also here to meet your cousin Giselle?"

"She would be expected soon?" she responded, not quite replying to his question.

"There is a meeting of the Norman Lindsay Society. She invited me to attend as a guest."

"I wouldn't want to interrupt your visit," she offered. "I will call her at our usual time."

Mira and her cousin met every few months over a meal in Seattle at the Queen Mary Tea Room. Sometimes they met up for the Seattle Art Walk as well, but that was none of his business.

"Lovely to see you, Uncle." Mira said breezily. "I heard about your arrangement with Gran," she said, attempting candor. "Over the duel..." she prompted.

His face suddenly turned ashen, his lips thinning, while his cheeks tightened.

"Who told you?" he demanded in a sudden and unexpected exclamation. "I'll have their hide."

In his rage and grief, he allowed his feelings free reign. He forgot to be as careful as usual. Mira couldn't resist fanning the fury, just to see what came out. No one in the family appeared to know about the details of the duel, let alone that Priam had been involved. It appeared he had been deliberately trying to avoid Mira as she and Gran had been close.

"It was not the first time you dueled," Mira reminded him. "Just the first time the balance required Gran to be," she paused for effect, "elsewhere."

"It wasn't supposed to end that way."

"And which way was that, dear Uncle?"

"With me owing her a favor," he complained, "and her not around to tell me how much trouble that's going to cost me," he continued. "I should have avoided the duel," he muttered.

He was vibrating with his feelings, though she was not sure why he was quite so upset. The air around him shimmered and small stones started jittering around his feet, small cracks appearing in the concrete of the step he was standing on. She felt that she had learned enough from him at this point, and wanted him to calm down before the lovely statues hereabouts suffered from the fallout of his ire.

"But we were just leaving," she indicated Edward, "much as I'd like to stay and chat." She walked across to the statue of the woman sphinx with a body and face of a woman, haunches, arms and tail of a lion, and turned her back to Edward for a moment. Looking her uncle directly in the eyes, she spoke quietly.

"We will be seeing each other soon, Uncle. Do not let us keep you." She waited while he gathered himself into some semblance of his usual impassive calm.

"Until we meet again. Do try to visit your family," he couldn't help adding as he walked towards the Gallery.

"Where to next, O Dragon?" she asked. She knelt to pick up a banksia blossom that had blown down alongside the path, putting it in her bag for later. She added a small piece of stone to her pocket collection at the same time. At this rate she would have a pocket full of places, tokens to travel on, Mira thought wistfully.

"Visiting your family would not be the worst idea." Edward ventured, back in hesitant mode.

"You only say that because you have a hopeful disposition," Mira quipped back.

"I only say that because it would be unexpected. The message from Argent seemed to indicate she had left you some information near where they reside."

"I hate it when everyone else is right," she admitted. Mira arranged backpack and messenger back more comfortably. He had offered to carry the backpack, but she felt more secure keeping her essentials about her. She centered, shielded and braced herself for the transition, bravely holding out her hand for him to grasp.

"I will be there with you."

That was actually comforting. Within the family home he didn't have to stay in human form. If they annoyed her, she could always try to persuade him to go all Dragon on their asses. She didn't ask how he knew where they were going. If he wanted her to know, he'd mention it.

"Let's do it," Mira said.

15

HOME COMFORTS

M eredith!" Edward exclaimed, as they arrived at her mother's house on the Oregon coast. The transit destination surprised Mira as it indicated he had been here before. "You look more beautiful all the time." A courtesy and sentiment that had the virtue of being true. If Mira aged like her mother, she'd be grateful for the genes. Her mother's elegant face was only enhanced by a streak of purple paint and a colorful paintbrush pushed absently behind one ear.

"Edward!" Meredith exclaimed. "I didn't know you knew my Miranda. What a welcome surprise."

"Mira and I only met recently," he replied. "I was inspired to bring her to visit your lovely self."

"A good choice" she responded, reaching out to pull Mira into her slender arms for a fierce hug. "I don't see you nearly often enough" she chided without any heat. "Come in, come in. I'll put on the kettle for a nice cup of tea."

Mira and the Dragon looked at each other ruefully. Their short acquaintance seemed to consist of tea, punctuated by conversation and journeys. She didn't have the heart to tell him that her whole life seemed similarly bracketed, with tea the only real constant.

Her mother's house was both rustic and comfortable, decorated in neutral creams and earth tones, punctuated by the dramatic splashes of color in jewel-toned rugs, cushions, and a startling collection of glorious abstract paintings on every available wall. They were the current batch of her mother's work, ones that had not yet found a home in a New York or London gallery, or the homes of an avid collector. The motion and color dynamics were breathtaking, with rich slashes of pigment, brush strokes overlaid on palimpsest, layered over delicate filigrees of paint as fine as spun sugar. Overall, they gave the impression of the impassioned conversation of storm and weather, mediated by angry gods, and blessed by moments of calm glory. As a painter, Meredith was a genius. As a mother and caregiver, Mira thought, not quite so brilliant.

"Wonderful!" Mira exclaimed, moving to examine a painting over the couch. It gave the impression of a peacock entwined with a fire bird, in the middle of a storm, with a single grace note of light shining down from a dark sky.

"That's The Embrace," Meredith said, bringing tea to the cluttered dining room table. A basket of colored yarn shared space with a half-sculpted gargoyle face, a sleeping orange tabby kitten and a jar of paintbrushes, soaking in turpentine. Meredith put the tea tray on top of some unopened bills and papers. Mira reached out to rescue a pencil draw-ing of the kitten from underneath the tray. "It's for the New York show in November. I think I may suggest they use it for the invitation."

"Miranda, please play mother." Meredith gestured for Mira to pour the tea for everyone. Her mother almost never called Mira by her nickname.

"Are you well?" she asked. "How is life in Seattle treating you?"

"Well enough," Mira responded "I have made some good friends, and Dr. Horrible is being his usual demanding cat self". She smiled ruefully, looking at a small scratch on her wrist. Dr. Horrible sometimes played like a kitten, and had given her a love pat across her hand. "I thought I'd look at that old trunk of my stuff while I am here."

"It's all up in your old room," she smiled. "It may be dusty, but I think Belladonna has been keeping things in order. I don't think I've been up there since the spring." Belladonna was a brownie who insisted on looking after her mother. It was one of her only concessions to the magical life she'd lived some thirty years ago, and only tolerated as they got along so well. "Busy," she added, waving her hand around the room at the paintings.

"If you don't mind?" Mira asked her mother and Edward.

"Don't mind us. We'll play catch up." Her mother turned to Edward "What have you been doing in the last couple of months?"

Mira was mildly surprised that Edward and her mother knew each other, especially as he was apparently so new to human form, but tried to put the puzzle aside. She was relieved she had the opportunity, and time alone, so she could rummage around in her old things. She had kept a journal back when she lived with Gran, and thought it might be in the bundle of keepsakes in the old steamer trunk. She was mainly surprised because it sounded like the Dragon had met her mother not long ago, sometime before coming to find her in Seattle.

16

MEMORIES

Mira took the stairs two at a time, taking pleasure in the familiar house, even though she'd always felt more like a visitor than a resident. Her mother tended to be preoccupied with whatever painting series was possessing her and had limited time for human interaction. They were lucky they'd arrived when she was taking a break between painting sessions.

She paused after opening the door. It was a comfortable room near the staircase, with its own window seat, walk-in closet, and a tiny bathroom. Just before going away to college, she had spent a long summer here, though she had been back infrequently in the last few years.

Everything was just as she remembered it, and if there was any dust, she couldn't spot it at first glance. Opening the closet, she spotted the old trunk in a corner, next to some old gardening boots and a flat box with some of her own workmanlike, but artistically unsuccessful, attempts at drawing. Oh, she did well enough with sketches of archeological digs, renderings of artifacts and the like. Not in the same league as her mother though. It still stung a little.

Living with great talent like her mother's art was a little tough on family, especially on the child-that-was.

The tumble lock on the trunk still yielded to the old combination, not changed since she was seven years old. Even though she had lived most of the time with Gran, Mira kept most of her keepsakes here at her mother's place. She was an infrequent and welcome visitor here, and her mother was delightful in her odd breaks from her art pursuits. Not a good caregiver, but that didn't make her love any the less fierce when she was paying attention. Her mother just tended to be absent-minded about small beings in her care. Mira was sure the kitten was being fed more by the brownie than by her owner. She shook her head and sighed internally, full of fondness for her brilliant artist that was her mum.

Mira removed a flat tray in the top, and found the pile of papers, school reports, and journals below it. Underneath was a small box she had forgotten. It contained some of her early talismans, and a faded ribbon with an old fashioned key on it that Gran had given her. Impulsively, she drew it over her head and tucked it into her shirt. It felt warm in her palm, and oddly reassuring. The journal took some rummaging; it had fallen to the side of the trunk, wedged into an old shawl.

Whispering a charm, she opened it to a random page. A drawing of a carved wooden cup looked out at her, with the legend carved around the rim of the cup "wish your will, drink your fill." She remembered Gran teaching her about the family wish magic, something she had not thought much about for years. The legend on the cup filled her eyes with tears for a moment. She reached up to wipe them away.

The book was only just bigger than her palm; she closed it and tucked it into a thigh pocket in her pants, buttoning the pocket closed. Putting back the tray, she picked up a lovely, sinuous carving of a dragon spirit from the flat tray. She'd take it to the Dragon. She thought he'd appreciate it. She also took a small, carved bamboo flute, tucking it into another cargo pocket on her outer thigh.

"There you are," Mira was greeted by her mother as she returned to the living room. "I was about to send out search parties." This she could safely ignore. It was a litany she'd heard so often as a child, it had rubbed mellow in her ears.

"You can take the Beemer if you're going run down the coast to visit your dad," she followed on. "I will be heading back to work, so if I'm not around when you get back, just leave the keys on the table." Mira was grateful for the offer. The Dragon had no reference location for her father's place, and a clear visualization was needed for translocation. As he was a little massive for her to move instantly, Mira thought it best to arrive by normal means.

"Thanks, mum. That'd be welcome," she said gratefully. "We'll be moving along, and let you get back to the Work."

17

ROAD TO PORTLAND

C ome along, Edward." Mira picked up the keys and her backpack, hugged her mother, petted the soft fur of the purring kitten, and headed for the door. "Daylight's wasting." It was well before noon, and they should be able to make Portland in a few hours.

"I'll drive for the first leg" she volunteered, throwing her pack into the back seat. The mellow dark chocolate of the custom paint job gentled her eyes, the leather seats of the BMW enfolded her in luxury that was very welcome after experiencing quite enough time transitions for one day. It would be good to travel at a more normal speed for a change.

Edward folded his tall form into the passenger seat, adjusting the angle of the seat.

"Did you find what you were looking for?"

"Not yet, though I found something that reminded me of you." She dug into her pocket, pulled out the little dragon carving, and passed it over to him. It was a bronze stained Chinese Dragon, curled around a golden ball. She had made it as a school project when she was trying sculpture and rather liked the face on it. It had a ferocious face, but the angle of the jaw suggested laughter.

"For me?" he asked hopefully.

"Be my guest."

He cupped his hands reverently around the little dragon, breathing on it gently. She fancied she could see a little wisp of white smoke curling from his nostrils.

"Thank you" he said reverently. "I will cherish something made by your hand."

Mira put the car in gear, and wound her way down the drive, beneath the canopy of trees over the road, and towards the connecting road to the interstate. They would arrive outside Portland in time for early afternoon tea, and could visit her father's family without being caught up in dinner plans. Perhaps there would even be an opportunity to visit Powells Bookstore later on; it was not outside the realm of possibility.

Portland was a lovely city for walking. The Southwest area had park blocks right through the center of the city, running in a strip of cool shade between restaurants Portlanders were justly proud of. She recalled the Saturday University Market with some fondness. She had a wonderful breakfast there last visit, with fresh biscuits and brown mushroom gravy. She had eaten it on a park bench, along with fresh lemonade. An old man in his eighties had shared stories with her while she ate.

She thought wistfully about visiting one of the fine restaurants on the way out of town. She did not think it would work out. Unlikely yes, but not impossible.

Reminded of the wishing cup, she focused her Will on her wish for safe travel and equally safe departure again, for a moment. No harm in it. And it may even balance some of her family's usual attempts to co-opt her to their benefit.

"Your mother's Art is magnificent" he said, out of the blue.

"Yes, it is."

"The energy of it reminds me of Norman Lindsay," he said unexpectedly. "Though her work is abstract, of course."

"That is perceptive of you," she responded. "The family story is that mom's family is distantly related to the Lindsay family, though I'd not noticed the energetic signature being so similar before. Perhaps it is seeing them in close time proximity that reminds me of the passion in both artists."

"There is something about the emphasis of the brush strokes," he ventured. "And perhaps in the quality of the light."

"Gran always said that a true artist was as powerful as a magician," she mused. "They see beneath the surface of the world, and challenge the norms of society."

"I can see that in your mother's work," he agreed. "The violence and color speaks to my Other form. Perhaps she will allow me to 'collect'," he said delicately "one or two works for my Hoard."

"I think she would be delighted to think of them gracing such a sterling location." She was teasing him a little. Some part of her imagined his Hoard as a cavern somewhere in a pocket universe, though no doubt he lived in some other-world aerie, a castle by any other name.

Edward looked pleased, and just a little smug, unaware of her imaginary dank cavern, adorned by precious paintings and piles of treasure, heaped into mounds of coins and crystal. She smiled inwardly, thinking she was treading on dangerous ground by teasing a Dragon about his Hoard. No laughing matter to a Dragon, or so she had read. In fact, there was seldom a more serious matter to a Dragon than their Hoard. And it was a rare matter indeed for a Dragon to mention which artifacts they would deign to include in such a collection. Her mother would be more than happy at the prospect of her work being chosen.

Mira decided the car trip would be a good time to find out what Edward thought about her uncle's reaction to their meeting.

"Edward?" she inquired. "Do you think my Uncle Priam overreacted when I mentioned the duel?"

"Hmmm. In what manner?"

"He seemed a little sensitive when I mentioned the terms of the duel."

"Sensitive? I thought he was going to burst a blood vessel."

"Well yes. Me too. But he seemed a little surprised to see me. I got the feeling he would have preferred to avoid me altogether," she said.

"You may have something there," he mused. "Do you think the future favor might be something you may be able to claim in Argent's absence?""

"I didn't even think of that," she said thoughtfully. "That may have something to do with his bad mood, though Jin Rael didn't mention it."

"Jin Rael may not have been close enough to the duel to catch those nuances."

"Well, that's something I can fish for information about. At the very least, it will annoy Jin Rael." Mira said gleefully. "I find that I'm annoyed enough about his knowledge of Gran's absence to want to make life difficult for him, if I can."

"Now you are starting to think like your Grandmother," he said approvingly. "She was never one to allow an advantage to slip from her grasp."

Just then, she noticed a sign by the side of the road that just said 'Big Tree'. That was intriguing. Mira wondered how big it must be to warrent the sign, especially as the surrounding forest had quite a few enormous trees in immediate view.

"Do you want to stop and look at the Big Tree?" she asked.

"Why not? It must be quite something to warrant its own special sign."

18

BIG TREE

They made their way onto the side road, stopping at a small dirt parking place. They got out of the car, pausing to stretch their backs and their legs. Following the signs alongside a trail, they soon came to a mossy clearing in the forest that contained one of the largest cedar trees Mira had ever seen. It was partly hollow on one side, the opening in the tree stretching up way over her head. The trunk of the tree seemed to be almost as wide as a medium sized house.

The size of it indicated it was ancient indeed, perhaps even part of the original old growth forest. Mira was both intrigued and curious. She felt invited to walk over and enter into the tree. The energy of the cedar seemed to beckon her in. She approached with reverence and stepped into the opening in the side of the tree.

When she turned around the clearing and the Dragon had disappeared, as had the opening in the tree. She found herself in a large open room, with wooden walls and a stone floor interrupted by tangled roots. The gentle glow of light had a greenish cast, illuminating runes on the arch of an open doorway to one side. From inside the arch over the doorway, light shone a little brighter, as if to encourage her curiosity. The runes over the arch were in the familiar script of the tablets from Nineveh. What they were doing here though in the Pacific Northwest, she could hardly imagine. She rather thought this was a place out of time, with the tree acting as a time anchor.

She felt a little dizzy and unbalanced. The complex scent of moss, cedar, and resin was strong here, together with a hint of mugwort and damiana. An odd combination to find in an ancient tree. Then again, an ancient tree had no particular business turning into a closed room either. She hoped the Dragon could hang on to his temper; a fire-breathing being getting annoyed with a tree could be fraught with misunderstanding.

She noticed a sound that had been present for a little while, but was now getting more persistent. It was a sound she had heard before, but Mira could not remember where she had heard it. Voices, hundreds of different voices, all speaking at once, a choir of voices chanting, singing, and droning in more than one language at the same time. The tones were rising and falling over the sound of bells and a drum-beat that echoed in her own heartbeat. The drum beat was becoming faster and more insistent, causing her own heart to speed up to match it. Her head pounded. She felt pressure in her ears for a moment and her eyes. And then it all stopped.

Silence.

The light beyond an arch brightened and pulsed. She moved towards the green light without thinking about it. The brightness became stronger, until she was nearly blinded by it. She blinked rapidly, shading her eyes with one hand as she moved forward. After one blinding pulse, the brightness lessened, becoming bearable. Wiping the tears from her eyes, blinking away the dazzle left in the aftermath of the light, she looked around her. The room was full of shelves, and the shelves were covered in books of various kinds. There were tablets, bound folios, scrolls, and some stacks of parchment. On a table in the middle of the room was a thick bound book on a tall pedestal. On the tooled leather cover, in Sanskrit of all things, a language in which she was fluent, was a legend. It read *The Rede of Trees.* Sumerian and then Sanskrit? Whatever next.

Now Mira was very confused. Had she walked into a tree, or had the tree walked into her?

Everything seemed inverted. She knew the Rede had once been a Library, part of the mysteries that were written on the inner bark of ancient trees, and preserved magically by the ancient gods. That much Gran had shared with her, before she had tesseracted it into a single Book, much like the one in front of her now. That book, however, had been magically transformed into a complex rune that had been inked onto her skin. Inked by Gran's magic though, and not with needles. She remembered it hovering like a small green glowing tree over her solar plexus, just before Gran had pressed it into her body. On her skin, it was a delicate tracery of pale green, gray and white, in a complex mandala that looked not at all like the tree it had been just moments before. The same symbol was on the cover of the book in front of her. Was she inside a tree? Inside herself? Inside the Rede?

Yeeesssss. Came a voice, echoing both within her head, and all around her in this space.

That was startling. But it seemed to fit the place. The voice was whispery, like the rustling of leaves or old papyrus.

Are you the Rede? she asked, a little hesitantly.

Not exactly. the reply came. *But you can call me that if you like.*

Why did you bring me here?

I have always been here came the response.

I mean here inside the tree? Mira asked.

Are you a tree? Mira was asked in turn.

Mira took a deep breath, and belatedly centered herself. This was very confusing. She tried again.

You are talking to me. Did you need to bring me here to do that?

You are becoming.

Becoming. Becoming a tree? Mira asked, bewildered.

Becoming. There was a pause before the voice came again.

Before you sleep, listen for me.

The light started pulsing in the room again, dimming gently until it was nearly dark. The outer room's green light was welcome to her eyes. She moved towards it, if moving was the right word. When she turned around again, the archway and the room of books was gone. She reached out a hand to the bark of the tree, snatching back her fingers quickly as the bark bit into them, a splinter lodging in the side of her middle finger. A sharp spike of sensation moved from her middle finger to settle in the palm of her hand.

Abruptly, the light of the forest beyond the tree flooded the space. The wall was gone. She stepped out of the tree to see Edward, pacing back and forth in the clearing. When he turned back in her direction, he seemed startled.

"Where were you?" he demanded. "You were here one moment and have been gone for at least ten minutes."

"Hmmm. I wandered around the back of the tree and got a tad lost. This bit of forest seems to have a mind of its own. Let's get back to the car," she said, heading in that direction.

Looking down, she could see a smear of blood on her finger where the splinter was lodged. It was a good thing she had a first-aid kit in the car so she could deal with it.

"You are bleeding," he accused. "Are you all right?"

"Just a splinter. I'm sure I'll be fine." She certainly hoped so. The experience would take some thinking about. She was none too happy about the blood sacrifice it had taken from her to release her back into the world. She was equally certain, in a way that felt real, that the experience had been engineered by the Rede to get her attention. Attention it had duly received.

It was time to get back to the car. Along the way, she noticed faint markings in the moss on the trees that bore the same silvery runes as she had seen over the arch in her vision experience. She didn't know if they were really there, or if it was an overlay in her vision that would fade in time. Either way, the world was changing around her and equally so within her. The changes were unfamiliar, however, and she did not want to talk to the Dragon about them. The only person she would have felt okay discussing this with was Gran, and she was inconveniently absent.

They swapped drivers when they got to the car. Mira pulled out the splinter, and doctored the small wound with some antiseptic and a dinosaur-printed child's bandage from her kit. She absent-mindedly put the splinter into a small empty jar and closed the lid.

"Do you mind if I take a nap for an hour?" she asked, feeling overwhelmed and a bit odd.

"Not at all. I'll wake you when we get closer to Portland."

Mira settled down in the passenger seat of the car, reclining it to a more comfortable angle. She set her mental clock to wake her in an hour. If she was going to have a living library chatting with her in vision, it was time to put her thoughts in order. She would put herself in memory trance, and recall as much as she could from her magic lessons with Gran as a child. It seemed she could no longer skate by on the Quiet Way, not if the Rede was anywhere near as dangerous and as desirable to those in power as she feared.

It was time to brush up on her skills, and to bring the Martial Way forward within her. It would give her more resources, though it would also make her more noticeable. However, The Quiet Way had been intended for the life of a quiet research librarian. This adventure had already made more demands on her than that. She was not entirely pleased with how things were unfolding. Still, Gran hadn't raised any stupid kids. No sense in ignoring what was right in front of her. Life was going to get all kinds of interesting. Her father's family would be pushing at her from the moment she arrived. It was past time for her to start pushing back.

19

THE MARTIAL WAY

Mira woke just as the car was pulling into a Starbucks parking lot, just at the outskirts of Portland.

"I thought we might stop for a hot drink and a snack," Edward said. "We've made good time."

"Good thought. I don't drink coffee; it smells much better to me than it tastes," she replied. "Starbucks has quite a good chai though. And you might like their chocolate chai."

Mira was feeling much better. Her head felt clear and the confusion she had been plagued with seemed to have disappeared. There was a new spring in her step as her body responded to the Martial Way, the discipline she had embraced while she slept. It changed her balance to lower in her belly and loosened shoulders she hadn't realized had become so tight again.

After they ordered and received their drinks, they found a table in a corner and watched the typical Portland crowd. A bike messenger sat with his helmet over the back of a chair. Two businessmen were sitting at a table with laptops, phones and papers, and a couple of cute girls were holding hands across the table, while they drank their lattes with their free hands. The barista was dealing with a running stream of drive-by customers, serving up drinks in the window to the drivers.

"Where is your father's place?" Edward asked. "I was going to wake you for the last part of the journey."

"The family owns an apartment building and adjoining office building downtown," she said. "They manage an investment firm that has offices around the world. My father is usually here in the summer and fall."

She took a sip of her hot chai tea latte, and a bite of the delicious cherry rhubarb tart. The flavors in the tart were rich and decadent, a combination of fresh fruit that was only available in the summer months.

"Do you mind if I introduce you as my 'friend', Edward?" she asked.

"I would be honored," he replied. "Do you think it best to avoid sharing information about my friendship with your grandmother?""

"Exactly!" she said. "My father's family can be a little tricky to manage. I generally try to avoid giving them too much information about my life."

"I understand completely. We will treat it like a Council reception, with all the undercurrents that usually entails."

She laughed wryly.

"I know. I know. You've been doing this kind of thing for longer than I have been alive."

"I bow to your experience with your family," he acknowledged, nodding his head. "I have not met any of them in this form, so we may proceed as you wish. Lord Priam recognized me only because I had met him in this form at the Residence at Library."

"Good. Thank you." She finished the last sip of her chai, prepared to make the last small drive to the family stronghold.

20

FAMILY CUSTOMS

They parked in the underground garage, using a key card Mira pulled out of a side pocket in her tapestry bag. The same key card gave them entrance to the secured elevator and, once inside, with a pin code, to the upper floors.

She didn't visit often though she noticed that the usual protocols were in place. When they arrived at the penthouse level, they exited in a quiet foyer, and took another door to the left. This door had a keypad as well as a scanner for the key card. Mira punched in a sequence of numbers, muttering a phrase under her breath. It always annoyed her to go through the security protocols here, though she supposed they were in place for good reasons, both business and magical.

A polite young man who was certainly more deadly than he looked, stood guard outside an ornate door. He nodded to Mira in recognition.

"Hello Paul," she murmured. "How is the mood in there?"

Paul nodded back.

"As usual," he responded, cryptically. "They will be pleased to see you. And your guest?"

"Ah, yes." She gestured Edward forward. "This is my friend, Edward," she added blandly. "We are traveling together."

"The Family is having cocktails in the small living room. Will you want to freshen up before joining them?"

"No need. They are used to me by now." It would annoy them for her to arrive in casual clothes, which is why she was going to do so. She enjoyed the small pleasure of bending the family rules. It would also give them something obvious to be annoyed with her about, and that might also be useful. Where her Family was concerned, she'd use misdirection to begin with, saving more overt action until later.

~~~

They were just a few steps past the door when a small child came barreling around the corner and ran into her legs.

"Whoa there," Mira said as she reached for the small sturdy body. The child's harried nurse came around the corner, following close behind the tornado of the child and the magical energy bound up in the running form.

"Won't!" the small form stated emphatically, stepping behind Mira. "Tell her she can't make me."

"Come along, Indi. Sorry for the fuss." The latter comment was addressed to Mira and Edward. "It is time for your nap."

"I'm *big*." The voice had a surprising degree of vibrato for such a small person. "Don't want to nap." The girl, for the voice was definitely female, stamped her small foot.

The Dragon unexpectedly knelt down on one knee, addressing the small form directly.

"You're very big for a cabbage," he said seriously, "and kind of small for a mountain." He paused, tilting his head to one side as he looked at her with one eye, then the other. "Are you becoming a mountain?"

The child giggled at him, diverted from her temper. She walked over and peered into his face intently.

"I can *see* you. You're bigger in your other body." He smiled at her and touched her nose.

"Quite right" he said. "I'm Edward. And who might you be?"

"I am Indi," she said gravely, "and I'm four."

"Yes, I can see that." He looked up at the nurse. "Perhaps she might stay with us, and we'll bring her back to you shortly." He looked back at Indi, saying "This is Mira."

Indi looked at Mira "Mirror. Mira. You're bad, like me? Everyone says so."

Mira laughed back at her.

"Is that what they say?" She turned to the nurse. "You may go." Mira reached out a hand to Indi, who put her own small hand trustingly inside it.

"Are you really my cousin?" Indi whispered.

"Yes, sweetie, I think that I might be."

Indi tugged on Mira's hand until she bent down to whisper in Mira's ear.

"Did you know he's a Dragon?"

"Shhhhhh. What makes you say that?"

She got an indignant look from her cousin.

"Well duh. I can *See* him. I can *See* lots of things I'm not supposed to," she stopped, saying seriously. "But momma doesn't like it that I *See*. So mostly I don't tell her." She peered into Mira's face. "You can *See* too?"

"Yes, I can," she added "It always got me into trouble too." Mira considered for a moment, before asking "Would you be okay with not telling that he's a Dragon?"

"Okay." Indi agreed willingly "Can I come with you?"

"Sure. We're going to the small living room."

"They'll be fighting about me again," Indi announced in her small voice. "That won't be much fun. Will you come see me later instead?"

"Sure, we'll come see you before we go." Mira said.

"Bye." Indi ran off in the direction she had originally come from.

"Quite the interesting child," said Edward quietly. "Who is she?"

"My Uncle Gavin's daughter. I'd heard there was some drama about or around her mother, but not the details. I think Gavin's going to have an interesting time with her. She reminds me of myself as a child."

"I would like to visit with her later," he said. "She is very bright with power."

"Later," Mira agreed.

~~~

M ira, darling!" her stepmother Elaine exclaimed. "You are here." She rushed forward in a froth of lace, perfume and kisses to both of Mira's cheeks. "And so fashionably informal." She turned to Edward "Who is your young man?"

"Lovely to see you. You look amazing, as always." Mira turned to the Dragon "This is Edward, a friend." She emphasized the last word, in vain hope that it would register. Elaine could be such a flutter-wit when something she didn't want to pay attention to presented itself.

"But of course he is." She embraced Edward too. "Come along and join us in the Salon." That was her preferred label for the smaller living room. Elaine's dark hair was pulled up into a tumble of curls, her long dress alternating layers of lace that was edged with ribbons, with yet more ribbons tied loosely along the narrow pleated bronze sleeves, in the style preferred at the Seelie court. Mira had a closet of such dresses here at the residence, for semi-formal family occasions. Unfortunately, most family occasions seemed to be conducted in a style that mimicked older customs and ceremonies.

"Look who I found!" Elaine exclaimed as they entered a room that seemed more crowded for the level of conversation in it. On second glance, there were only a dozen people present. Their entry halted the various heated exchanges occurring near the fireplace. Her father, two uncles and their spouses, Aunt Helena and her protégé, Alexander, two of her cousins, Artemisia and Rowan, a man of about thirty with blond hair in a suit, and her brothers Iain and Kevin.

Her father walked over to join them.

"Miranda." He grasped her by both shoulders, and squeezed, lightly, before letting go. This was what passed as a hug for him.

"And your friend?"

"Father, this is my friend, Edward." She turned towards Edward. "Edward, this is my father, Henry Ambrose."

"Pleased to meet you, Sir," said Edward diffidently, playing the youth meeting elder statesman. She smiled inwardly. She was quite sure the Dragon was some ages older than her father, even if her father did lay claim to several millennia.

"I am familiar with your monograph on the *Contingencies of Financial Power in Medieval Venice*," said Edward. That surprised her, and also, apparently, her father. His study on financial power in Venice was a classic work on brokering deals and raising capital in dangerous political circumstances. However, it was only well known in financial circles.

Her father glanced at her.

"Your taste in friends has improved," Henry said. "What can I get you to drink?"

"A glass of champagne for me," she requested, "and for you, Edward?"

"If you have a Single Malt Scotch that you favor, that would be pleasant."

"Indeed. An 18 year McCallan suit you?"

"Splendid."

Conversation started up again, interwoven with greetings. The argument seemed to settle around young Indi, and whether she should go to stay with her mother in the

Dark Court, or be trained in magic along with her cousins here in Portland. Her abilities were a mesh of both worlds, surprisingly strong to be showing up in one so young. There was concern that in the Dark Court her ability to See would expose her to too many terrors. Indi's mother Ninian was, surprisingly, arguing against Indi being with her at the Dark Court, while her father was arguing the opposite viewpoint.

Exasperated, Mira cut across the argument, "Why don't you ask Indi where she wants to be?"

"She's only four, Mira" said her brother Kevin, "and she will go where she is told."

"Only if you want her dead or insane before she reaches five," she said quietly, stating in her direct fashion what they'd all been dancing around. That earned her a grateful glance from Ninian.

"Her cousins may be too much for her, if she stays here." Gavin argued. "I want her to be safe."

"She will soon be more dangerous than they are. If they have the sense of an animal cracker, they'll notice. Mess with her now and she will get even." Mira commented caustically.

"Like you did, Mira?" Iain chimed in. "I still have a scar from where you pushed me off a cliff when you were not much older than Indi."

"Never underestimate small girls." Mira smiled with gleeful malice. "You eventually learned how to fall." She looked around at the bunch of them, annoyed that they were so self absorbed. "If you don't ask her what she wants, I suspect you will deserve what she will turn into."

"Voice of experience?" asked Ninian as an aside.

"Me? I turned into a librarian." Mira claimed, not entirely accurately. "Not the same thing at all." She avoided her family partly to avoid them finding out what else she had turned into.

"It could all settle out by the time she's a teenager." Mira said.

"You had Gran to go stay with, love," said Kevin. He'd always been her favorite brother. She almost never felt like killing him. Unlike Iain. Though she wished he hadn't brought up Gran. That was a topic she would much rather avoid as long as possible.

Mira shrugged.

"I met her just now, when we came in. Indi, that is." She grinned at them. "I told her I'd come visit later, or she'd be here making her opinion known."

"Rotten little meddler you are," declared Kevin affectionately.

"I get it from my family," she agreeably nodded in his direction, raising her glass in salute.

Her father frowned at them both, as he usually did when they acted like brats.

"What would you do, Mira?" Ninian asked.

"Me? Not being a parent, I don't really have a say. However, I'd venture her mother has a point about the Court." She raised her eyebrow at Ninian. "Though I don't have context, I'm guessing there is some specific danger you would like to avoid?"

"Finally. Someone who asks, rather than pontificating." Ninian sounded relieved. "I have been called home by the Queen, an obligation that I cannot, and do not wish to, avoid. If there is some..." she paused delicately, "difficulty, it would be better to arrive without a ready hostage in tow." She sounded troubled. "I have no reason to think anyone would harm a child, precious as they are to all of us, but the circumstances are uncertain."

"Gotcha. And Indi has powerful potential, as well, though likely without much tact about it," Mira added.

"Exactly. She may See and say something that could be less than fortunate."

"Sounds like her momma's got a point there, guys." She gestured around at her clan. "Even if Uncle Gavin doesn't find it particularly convenient to be responsible for Indi himself," Mira said pointedly.

On that note, Mira drank the last of her champagne and turned her back on them to go get a refill. "Are you sure that was wise?" Edward asked, just a step behind her.

"My family rarely inspires wisdom," she replied. "Though they can occasionally be entertaining."

"I am also concerned about the small one." he said. "Will she be safer with her father?"

"Well, for definitions of safe, I wouldn't call Gavin all that and a pint of milk. Too caught up in business stuff to pay much attention. He also has the old-fashioned notion that kids are women's work."

"Will she get the training she needs in the *Sight*?" asked Edward.

"She will if I have anything to say about it," Mira said with some heat. "I'll have a few words about replacing the nanny, and will ask Jin Rael if he would care to look in on her. Jin Rael has a soft spot for children, and a particular fondness for those who have the *Sight*." Mira filled her glass while considering options. "It looks like I may also need to find some time to give Indi's cousins a talking to, and give Indi herself some pointers."

"Will her father consider that interference?" he asked.

"Likely. But they're accustomed to me making a nuisance of myself when I turn up." She paused in thought. "He'll just roll over and think I'm doing women's work by taking care of things. I'll chat to Ninian and see how she'd feel about me taking an interest."

Mira looked across the room at Ninian, reaching out with subtle energy to draw the fae woman's attention. Within a couple of moments Ninian excused herself and joined them at the bar.

"You had some thoughts?" she asked.

"Yes. If you don't think it too much meddling, I could teach Indi a couple of things that may help with her cousins?"

"Would you? That would be welcome. Though as you have only just met her, you should know she can be a handful," Ninian warned, cautiously.

"I also have a friend who is good with small children..." Mira suggested. "I could stop by periodically, and he could also look in on her as well if you agree." The look of relief on Ninian's face was worth the irritation of Mira having to deal with family more often. "Perhaps the nanny could be replaced with one who has more Will?" Mira continued.

"Thank you for your help, Mira. I have been getting to the very end of my patience. This is the first time anyone in your family has offered a reasonable thought towards a solution." Her voice became husky with emotion. "I never thought to have a child. I want her to be powerful, but I also want her to be safe."

There, that was the rub with this family, Mira thought. It was always about power first, last and always. You could not afford to be less than powerful, or they would try to run your life for you. She had been in Indi's position as a kid; as a child, she had too much magic of the wrong kind for the family, and too little sense of how vulnerable that made her. It was as well that Gran had stepped in for Mira. Mira felt she could do little else than step in to help where Indi was concerned. It felt a bit like balancing out Gran's help. Now she'd need to sell it to Gavin, and he was a bit block-headed.

"What are you plotting?" Gavin demanded belligerently, as she approached. "I doubt you decided to grace us with your presence to solve our child care issues." He pushed his energy at Mira, trying to use influence to get her to back down. His energy slid off her aura harmlessly. There was something in her own magic that made her resistant to magical manipulation.

"Just trying to help out, Uncle Gavin." Mira pushed back at him, using his own magic to slide past his barriers.

"Mira is going to look in on Indi for me," Ninian said softly, touching his chest in a caress, distracting him from his annoyance. "We will work something out that will be agreeable." Mira was sure there was more going on than a simple caress, as he abruptly capitulated. She looked at Ninian with respect. Her fae influence joined to Mira's magic, was stronger than the magic Gavin could wield.

"Fine then." He still sounded a little aggrieved. "See that you do." Gavin strode over to the other side of the room.

"That was interesting," Edward noted.

"How did you do that," asked Ninian. "He's been immovable all day.""

"Me? I'm sure it was your loving touch," Mira deflected. "I'll make a couple of calls, but I think I know of a good basic magical teacher who could double as a nanny for a while. An old teacher of mine, Mrs. Minsky, may be available. Or she may recommend someone." Under her breath, Mira muttered a charm to divert Ninian's attention to the solution rather than the awkward question of Mira's influence on Gavin. Her family seldom noticed her manipulation. Mira had a notion that Ninian was more sensitive to the nuances of magic.

Her father approached, with all the finesse of a shark cutting through the room. His energy was a bass rumble to her senses, though not as deep a rumble as the unheard thunder of the Dragon. It amused her that Edward had pulled in his energy field tight against his skin and was showing a rather mild friendliness in his aura. Good work that, and something she ought to emulate before her father got any closer.

"Father." She smiled brightly up at his six feet five inch height. "Such a lovely gathering."

"What are you doing here, girl?" he went right to the point. "You don't show up that often, and when you do, you stir things up."

"I love you, too." Mira grinned at him. "You'd get bored with the usual arguments if I didn't show up every so often."

"True. True. But this time I was expecting you." He looked very pleased with himself.

"Really? And are you planning to tell me why that is?"

"Eventually," he shot back, part of their usual dance. They secretly liked each other's style, but the steps of the dance needed to be followed. "You first." Well that at least was familiar. He always wanted to have all the information he could get, before he would share.

"I ran into Uncle Priam this morning," she stated. "The topic of his last duel with Gran came up in the conversation..." she waited, watching his face carefully. He was not surprised about the duel, but he did appear surprised that Mira and Priam had run into each other.

"I thought he would be avoiding you," he sallied.

"Well, we did meet at Norman's Pool, which is pretty far out of the way," she acknowledged.

"Interesting venue."

"It was a rather unexpected meeting for both of us," Mira offered. "He did appear perturbed when I mentioned the duel."

"I should think so. He ended up owing you a future favor from it."

"Me? I thought the loser owed the winner the future favor?"

"Your Gran couldn't afford to owe a future favor, so she made sure to win. But that meant she needed to leave this particular life. It remains to be seen how long she is away."

"It has been five years," she responded, "I came to ask why this is getting stirred up now?"

"Your Gran left instructions that take effect if she is away for more than five years," he admitted, "and that's going to have some impact on the family." He looked around at the gathering. "We should talk privately."

"As you like." She touched Edward's forearm for a moment as she addressed him. "Do you mind if I leave you alone for a short time? Father and I need to talk."

"Not at all. Please call for me if I can be of assistance." She nodded agreement before leaving with her father, both of them heading for his study, the place where the more private family business traditionally happened.

23

A STUDY IN MISDIRECTION

Three of the study's walls were covered in floor-to-ceiling bookcases. The books were an eclectic mix of finance, human law, magical grimoires, and historical texts. She expected the rarer books to be out of sight, and was not surprised to find that to be the case. The deep leather chairs were a bit too plushy and comfortable lulling visitors into a false sense of comfort. Mira liked to kick off her boots and curl up; her father usually thought this gave him an advantage. It was a feeling she was happy to encourage.

She always expected her family to twig to the way her peculiar magic worked, but they never seemed to. Each of them followed their usual practice of using manipulation magic, secure in the notion that it would work as expected. She let them get on with it, equally secure that their magic would bounce of her like rubber, and allow her to follow the signal back to stick her own influence to them like glue.

As the magic felt like their own, was in fact their own energy, they didn't notice the little bit of extra push she added to keep herself free of unwanted influence. And if that meant she was manipulating them? Well, she figured they started it.

Settling into a comfy black armchair near the fireplace, she accepted a dark Scotch from her father.

"Thanks," she sipped gratefully. "This is the good stuff."

"Do you have some thoughts about Uncle Priam, then?" she asked, knowing there had been no love lost between those brothers for years now. It was not unheard of for them to declare truce from time to time, however, by no stretch of the imagination could she see them trusting each other. She could barely see them trusting each other to engage in betrayal, double dealing, influence peddling, and general mopery and dopery. It came with the territory in this family.

"That terrible old woman has put us all in a difficult situation," he said, referring to Gran.

"What arrangements were you referring to earlier?" Mira asked. She was intrigued to know what mischief Gran had gotten up to this time around.

"She held a special place on the Council for a few millennia, from when she started it all," he replied. "Now she's designated you as her alternate, holding proxies and assigns."

"She's what?" Mira was surprised. "That's bound to annoy more than a few of the Council members."

"Not to mention having an impact on the family," he said quietly. "So, are you saying you didn't know about this until now?"

"No. This is a bit surprising to say the least," said Mira honestly. "How does this impact things with Uncle Priam?"

"Being her designate means any promises owing to Gran now accrue to you instead." Gran was his many times Great Grandmother too, something Mira always conveniently ignored. Several members of the family likely expected those assigns and proxies to come to them instead.

"Did you expect that to happen?" Mira asked. "You are in the direct line."

"I didn't expect the bloody minded old meddler to make herself absent in the first place," he said with exasperation. "She was annoying enough when present in the center of things, but she's even more inconvenient when absent."

"She always did like to keep people on their toes," Mira said fondly. She'd always liked the energy around Gran, and the way in which events coalesced to her advantage. Mira had very much missed Gran this last five years.

"It was always clear you were a favorite," affirmed her father. "Though I think she's stirred up a hornet's nest this time."

"By making plans that took five years to come to light?" Mira thought he was making too much of it. "I'm not sure I like the implication that putting me in the middle of things stirs things up."

"That's not the only thing she's put into play," he said. "If that were the case, I'm sure you would do your best for family interests." Mira thought he was too hopeful if he thought she would be making decisions that gave the family any particular advantage. Not without thinking through the balance of forces first.

"Five years is a mere moment in time to most of us who've been around for a while." He was playing with a disk of metal that had been old when Greece was a new civilization which she guessed made his point.

"I'm none too pleased to be put in the middle of things," Mira stated acidly. "What else do I need to know about?"

"There's a vote coming up that will change the balance in this World," he said, still not telling her what she needed to know.

"Okay, I'll play." Mira said. "You want to tell me about the vote?" Sooner or later, she would get him to answer the question about Uncle Priam. Though not until she'd heard what else he was concerned about.

"The Others are split into a couple of camps about whether to let the human's know what, if not exactly who, we are. There is some fear that they will welcome us on the one hand, or try to make war with us on the other."

"That discussion has been going on for some time now." Mira pointed out. "Gran talked about it as one of the eternal boring arguments in Council."

"Yes, but Argent had a unique perspective," he said. "She was in a position of influence with most of the groups, and related in some way which she never explained, to all of the Others." He paused, waiting to see if Mira had a reaction to that information. Her dear parent was still fishing for information.

"Gran was related to everyone," she responded. "We're all descended from her through one line or another." Didn't everyone know that?

"Did she happen to mention what she would do if knowledge of the Others came out?" he asked, sounding concerned.

"Gran always said it would come out sooner or later, and the most we could do was to choose our timing in the right way. I think she had some thought of cultivating various human groups like the United Nations, but thought they lacked power."

"There's bound to be trouble over it," he said. "The Winter Court is talking about making an announcement through one of the pharma lobby groups, and not waiting for the Council."

"That's likely why Ninian is being called home."

"Hmmm. Likely indeed."

"What is the angle for the pharmaceutical lobby?"

"I heard they're promising life extension techniques for corporate and political interests." He sounded annoyed. "And to make the techniques available to big pharmaceutical companies so they can market it."

"That would do it," she said. "Though they will be pressed to deliver against the demand."

"I suspect they're hoping to come out in a limited way, and with glamour fully on stun."

"They could start with a really exclusive spa in Washington, and promote it through the insider networks." Mira was certain something like this must be among the plans. The Winter Queen had been paying attention to human politics for some time. When she and Gran visited with them some ten years ago, conversation was already starting to swing in that direction. The Seelie healers had some skills with, if not reversing, then extending life, while smoothing out the wrinkles and marks of age in a surface way. Mira had the impression that the seeming of youth would be a big selling point in getting the glitterati behind the general Seelie agenda. She thought that setting up a spa on the West Coast would likely follow East Coast lobby efforts.

"What lobby is Uncle Priam working with?" she asked out of the blue.

"He is also interested in pharmaceutical companies, though mostly in the area of fertility," he said darkly. "He would like to own a couple of the big fertility companies. As a way of controlling human population in part, but also to look into declining Other birth rates."

"Out of the goodness of his heart, no doubt?" she said, somewhat sarcastically.

"You should start considering how you would like to leverage the future favor he owed to Argent and now owes to you."

He walked over to the bar to get another Scotch. Coincidentally, that put his back to her, so she could not see his face. His shoulders, however, were noticeably tight. That meant she could expect him to have some ideas of his own about how he would like her to use the favor for the family interests.

"And your interest in the pharma lobbies?" she asked. "Don't you have a controlling interest in several of the research and development labs in Seattle?"

"Yes, but those are mostly factored around cancer research. I need to diversify."

"Well that explains part of Uncle Priam's interest in avoiding me." Mira said. "When is this vote coming up?"

"Some time in the next few months", he said "which is a relatively short time away. Council would need to be summoned first."

"And the rest of Gran's inheritance?" she asked gently.

"Her assistant, an annoying young man called Jayson or Justin, came to see me this week at the office," her father admitted. "He said he was looking to get in touch with you about an inheritance. Did he catch up with you this week?"

"I hope you didn't tell him where I was." Mira chided.

"Not at all. He seemed to know you are located at a library in Seattle, but not at which library. I did not feel any need to help him narrow that down," he said.

"Good. I want to avoid him."

"Like you ignore everything from our world?"

"Not exactly," she said firmly. It was more that she wanted to keep her distance. She wished he'd understand. "Just until I work out what steps I want to take."

"Well, when you work that out, don't forget your family," he stressed. He tossed his drink back, reached for the bottle and gestured to offer her another drink as well.

"You know we're here to help and advise you."

Right. Like that was going to happen. She could just imagine the strings that would come with the so-called help. Still, her father had some good insight into the Council, and the players—she might need to be stopping by anyway to look in on the child, Indi. Keeping up with his views may not cost her too much if she was careful.

She could feel him wrapping his magic around the glass of Scotch he offered her, his energy reaching out to wrap her in influence. That is what she had been waiting for. She gently sent a wish back in his direction, along with the desire that he find her agreeable, and the conversation unmemorable.

It was time to get out of here and confer with the Dragon. Edward was bound to have his own views on the politics of the situation, and he was, so far, much more trustworthy than her family. At least he'd shown himself to be direct with her so far. However, she had not probed further for his own interests. He had been backing her plays with the family and acting as Gran's perfect messenger. Time to find out where he stood on the Others coming out to the world.

"Mira, darling girl. Do you know what happened to your Gran's personal library?" her father asked, expecting her to be influenced by the magic laced into her drink and the room.

"Hmmm? I expect it will be with her rooms when I go catch up with the Council," she suggested, quite sure he didn't mean the regular library. It was, ultimately, all Gran's library.

"There's something I'd like to see. Young Justin was also looking into it. It is called the Rede of Trees." He paused. "Do be a good girl and keep an eye out for it."

"Of course," she agreed. "I will pay particular attention to the library, and to the Rede of Trees." It would do no harm for him to think she was going along with him. And it had the virtue of truth. She would, indeed, pay attention to the library and the Rede of Trees, just not in the way he expected.

"Good. Do let me know what you find out."

"It's time we were leaving soon. I did want to stop by and see young Indi before we go."

"Her rooms are on the north side of the tower," he offered, helpfully. "You will find her in the green room."

"Good. That's near my old rooms. I'll stop by there for a bit." She put down her glass, reached out to kiss him on the forehead. "Keep well, father."

"I always do" he responded. "I'll be working on some business for a while. Do say goodbye to your brothers before you go."

24

LIGHTLY SINGED

Mira made her way back to the Salon to pick up Edward, as she thought a certain young girl would like a visit from him too.

"Is everything all right?" Edward asked when she found him leaning against the wall, watching the room unobtrusively. He had pulled shadow around himself, which likely made it difficult for the Family to pay much attention to his presence. It must have been an interesting hour, she thought.

"Just peachy," she said brightly. "Let's go find Indi before we head back to the coast."

~ ~ ~

"Mira. Mira." Indi jumped up and down on her bed, treating it like a trampoline.

"Hi poppet." Mira, not trying to stop the energetic child from exercising her Will. She would get enough members of the family trying to do that. Besides, Mira liked her spirit.

"Do you remember Edward?" Edward entered the room behind her, carrying shadow with him.

"There you are. You're shiny and dark." Indi announced. "And you sound like big bells."

Mira wondered where she had heard big bells for comparison. Personally, she thought he sounded like a jumble of brass instruments all playing at the same time, but she'd go with big bells as a fair description.

Edward rumbled with deep laughter, catching Indi up in mid leap, swinging her around and around in a circle before putting her down again.

"You are very shiny yourself, young lady." He tapped her on the nose. "Though perhaps only as loud as a saxophone." He waved his hands in the air, sketching out the shape of a saxophone in amber light that held the shape for an instant before dissipating.

"Do it again," Indi said. "Again." He complied, acting for all the world as though being an entertainment for small girls was the whole of his purpose in life. Mira grinned at him, approving of his actions. He may well be a bloodthirsty Dragon, but as a man he was a friendly sort. If a bit scattered and clumsy, such as when a shape he was making to amuse Indi tumbled slightly and singed the lampshade, she thought to herself.

"Okay, enough you two," she said. "Indi, how would you like a different teacher instead of the nanny?"

She got frowns in return. "Don't know." Indi muttered.

"It's my very own teacher, Mrs. Minsky" coaxed Mira. "She will teach you magic stuff," she followed "and a trick or two to play on your cousins." That got her attention.

"Will you come visit me?" she asked.

"Sure" Said Mira. "And your mother will be back from time to time as well."

"Okay. I like the idea of tricks."

"Good. I liked them too," said Mira. "Just remember you can *see* much better than your cousins can, and that will let you see their magic so you can push it back at them." Tucking her in, they headed back to the Salon for a final word with Ninian and Mira's brothers, before hitting the road.

The crowd in the Salon were still engaged in the same conversations. They had the sound of well-rehearsed positions, reiterated over more than one cocktail hour. Her brothers were arguing over the merits of influencing drivers in a car race versus wishing on horses at the track. It was a distinction that mostly ignored the sapience of the former, or the bloodlines of the latter. Not a new conversation for them.

Ninian and Gavin were in an intense, but quiet conversation over near the fireplace, and her cousins were discussing the benefits of cosmetics versus using magical coloring when attending a music event or dressing for a dance club.

Mira hugged her brothers, telling them to avoid getting into trouble, a vain hope at best. Interrupting Ninian and Gavin, she walked into the middle of their space.

"Hey guys, sorry to interrupt." She waited until she had their attention. "I checked in on Indi, and will get my old teacher over this way next week to get her some special tutoring." Gavin had been arguing again for Indi to go with her mother to the Court.

"Leave it alone, Gavin." She pushed at him, magically. "I was of similar age when Gran took me to the Court," she explained, "and it was only Gran's influence that got me out again safely." She paused to let Gavin catch up with what that meant. "So leave it. She's staying here."

"Ninian", she grasped her hands "let me know if I can help further. She's a good child. You must be proud of her."

"I am. I appreciate your care," she said formally, acknowledging the arrangements they had decided on together.

As they left, she waved to Paul. "Don't work too hard," she said.

"Come along Edward, let's hit the road."

25

THE HOLLOW ROAD

The trip back to her mother's place on the coast was uneventful. It was too late to visit Powell's Bookstore on the way out of town, which was disappointing. Though, there would be time for another visit. If she'd be back this way to look in on Indi, perhaps the next time she could visit the bookstore first, before family. Books were her passion.

The road had been blessedly free of traffic, and they'd taken advantage of the clear roads by opening up their sped a bit. Not enough to endanger other motorists, and with a wish to avoid being noticed by random highway patrol cars, yet satisfying to have the road under the wheels and the distance open in front of them.

As they reached the coast, sunset painted the sky in reds and purples ahead of them. It felt like the sky was rushing down to greet them, with a thin line of darkness hallowing the valleys and fields either side of the road.

"I hope my mother is seeing this sky," Mira said. She would love it."

"Her paintings are very fine," he replied. "I imagine she lives out this way in part due to the quality of the light."

"Not a bad guess. She says something similar about the light."

"I hope we will not be disturbing her when we arrive close to dark." He sounded concerned.

"Not at all. I expect I'll cook some dinner and set up the guest room for you. My mother will appear at some point, bolt some food, and get back to painting." She looked at him wryly. "She doesn't notice much about regular life when she's painting."

"We could go back to the islands tonight instead?" he suggested.

Mira pulled into the driveway, parking the car in the garage before turning to him. "I have some things I'd like to do here in the morning," she responded. "It would be good if we could stay until then."

"If you are certain," he agreed, a little doubtful of his welcome, "then of course we should stay."

"Mother" she called out as they entered the kitchen. "We're back." When there was no reply, Mira tossed her backpack on the couch. "Make yourself at home while I rustle up dinner."

In the refrigerator, she found a couple of sealed zip-lock containers with prepared meals, courtesy of her mother's housekeeper. However, after the long drive, she felt like making a curry. Something hot and savory would be welcome, and she thought Edward was looking a little hollow as well. "Curry okay with you?" she asked.

"I think so," he replied, gesturing at his lanky form. "I am not really accustomed to thinking about feeding this form. It seems inconvenient to need to feed more than once in a week."

She laughed.

"If you try that with a human form, you're going to fall flat on your face. Trust me."

"I will be guided by your experience." He said.

Mira laughed again.

"That's a fine turn of events. I suppose at some stage you will share your experience with me." She arched her eyebrows at him. "I have met a Dragon or two in my short life," she suggested. "And none of them were as agreeable,'" she paused, "or as mild in their opinions," another waggle of the eyebrows, "as you are presenting yourself to be."

Mira left him stretched out on the larger of the two sofas, and made herself at home in the kitchen. She quickly found the spices she had accumulated on previous visits where she expected to find them. Putting a heavy wok on the stove, she quickly chopped onions, mild peppers, mushrooms and potatoes, putting each in their own bowl until she was ready for them. Heating oil, she added mustard seed, stirring quickly as it sizzled, followed by coriander, turmeric and black pepper. When those were popping well, she added the onions and turned down the heat. She wanted the onions to caramelize, not burn.

Next came the potatoes, as they would take the longest to cook. She'd chopped them finely, which ought to cut down on the cooking time. Fossicking in the pantry was a little like spelunking. Hidden treasures were to be found in the depths of the capacious walk-in storage area, including chocolate buttons, which gave her ideas about a fine chocolate mousse for dessert. She grabbed them just in case, along with the coconut cream she had been searching for.

The dish was coming along nicely. Mira loved one-dish meals quite a lot, liking the way the flavors combined, with the colors nicely bright. She added the green, red and yellow chopped peppers, giving them a brisk stir, along with curry powder and a little more pepper once she tasted it. Last, she added the mushrooms, some water and white vinegar, along with half a jar of peach jam she found lingering on the door of the refrigerator. It always surprised Mira when friends paid through the nose for chutney. The difference between jam and chutney was basically a slug of vinegar, so she combined them in the dish instead. Cooking with fruit, vinegars and spices made dishes she could create in under half an hour, and gave her a core set of recipes she could tinker with endlessly.

Once the mushrooms had been added, she opened the can of coconut cream and stirred it in, turning the golden curry mixture into a rich, deep aromatic sauce. Her mother kept frozen packets of rice in the freezer; Mira grabbed one and microwaved it for three minutes. She could have started from scratch with the rice, but she felt lazy today. That's partly why her mother kept the freezer stocked. Mira usually topped up the freezer with tasty snacks her mother could eat quickly when the creative juices were flowing. Otherwise, she'd live on toast and cereal in the midst of painting frenzies.

Mira felt like her mother's painting trances were at least as complex as the magical work Mira and her father's family engaged in. To her vision, the energy whirling around both activities felt surprisingly similar. Most of the Others had an appreciation for Art. They were just not focused on creating it, unlike Mira's mother's extended, eclectic, and artistic clan. In a strange way, she mused, they both occupied worlds out of step with the mundane.

Serving up a bowl of rice and curry, Mira walked to the door into her mother's studio, but didn't venture further than the small entry area.

"Mother" she called softly. "There's curry when you get hungry." She placed the bowl on a table just inside the door, along with a cool drink of iced water infused with peppermint leaves. Happily, curry tasted nearly as good when it grew cold.

"Thank you dear," Meredith said. "I'll take a break soon, once I've got the sky blocked in."

Mira smiled fondly at her absent-minded parent, walking back through the passageway to the living room. It may be minutes, though experience told her it could be a couple of hours, before her mother surfaced again.

26

CONVERSATIONS

L et's eat at the table, Edward."

She served them rice and curry in red, shallow, glazed bowls, accompanied with sprigs of mint on the edge of the dishes, along with some apple sauce as a balance for the spicy, sweet flavors. Long, cold ice water glasses with mint were the finishing touch.

She pushed the kitten's nose away from investigating the curry.

"Not for you little one. This is human food." She plunked the kitten down next to the dry food, garnering a look of outrage.

"Okay, stinky cat food for you." She capitulated, opening a tiny can of tuna for him. "You're welcome," she said as the kitten ignored her in favor of the food.

"Are you ready to talk about your father?" Edward asked, sliding the question into the silence between bites of the delicious curry.

"It all comes back to Gran," she replied. "And the schemes of some very powerful interests in the Council. I don't know why she put me in the middle of it all."

"She always held you in the highest regard," he offered. "Partly because you do not seek to put yourself in the middle of things."

"What's that got to do with it," Mira complained. "She knew I had walked away from the family pursuit of power and influence."

"Exactly my point," he said. "And unlike Priam, she trusted you with the things she found most precious. The knowledge of the ancient forests, the hidden paths, the secrets of ancient dynasties – all of those would be simply a means to power for Priam, and for other members of your Family." Mira looked aghast at this assessment, though she could not disagree. She even agreed with his implicit capitalization of the word 'family'.

"My interest is in knowledge for its own sake, for seeking the mysteries, for love of the invisible splendors, for the liminal, the unseen, and for the little mysteries. I love the magic in the spoken and written word, the recording of slow thoughts." She gestured with her hands, shaping the air in intricate patterns, reaching out splayed fingers, as if to grasp the knowledge she spoke of.

"That is remarkably similar to the way Argent described her own path, and it is part of what makes you such a good candidate as the custodian of the Rede."

"Candidate? Is there a rite of passage needed? Can I give the Rede back? Give it up?" Words tumbled over themselves as she asked the questions, breathless at the possibility of making a different choice.

I am always here. she heard the Rede whisper softly, inwardly. *Don't you want to be with me?* it added with a sad lament in the inner voice.

"What just happened?" asked Edward. "You went away, and your energy shifted. What did you think of?"

"It is the Rede" she admitted, suddenly deciding to trust him a little more. "It speaks to me sometimes."

Edward looked at her big shoulder bag, seeming to think that the voice came from there, from one of the books she had been so careful to avoid him looking at too closely.

"Is that not an indication that Argent chose you wisely?"

"You didn't answer my question," she accused. "Do I have the choice to put this down?"

"Yes," he said, "Also no." he replied. "It depends on what you think of as choice."

"Gah! Stop sounding so cryptic," she grumped, "you great annoying lizard."

"Dragons are not related to lizards" he replied, standing on his dignity. "We are born of time and storm, made flesh in the wonderment of stars."

"And so aren't we all?" she asked.

"Some of us more than others," he said, standing on his dignity.

"Children, children," came the chiding sound of her mother's voice. "You will give the kitten bad dreams." She put on the kettle in the kitchen and joined them at the table.

"So what's this all about?"

They glanced at each other, each wondering how much to tell her.

"Out with it, Miranda!" Meredith said, in a rare focus of attention on the here and now.

"Gran left me a rare part of her library," she started, "to mind for a while."

"And then left you holding the bag?" asked her mother. "You should have known better."

"She said she needed to hide it for a while," said Mira, "and I thought I was helping."

"She's a manipulative old woman, and she knows you too well," said her mother. "Whatever made you think she would come back for it?"

"She didn't exactly say she would come for it," Mira mused. "She did say she would send someone to help."

"And I suppose that's where the Dragon comes in?" he looked startled that she recognized his true nature in human form.

"Oh please!" She exclaimed. "I noticed the first time you arrived." She looked him up and down, lingering on his eyes. "I'm an Artist." She turned to Mira.

"Why do Others always think I won't notice what they are?"

"I don't know." Mira said. "Perhaps because you're human?"

"Human?" questioned Edward. "She's no more human than you are." It was her mother's turn to be startled.

"What makes you say something so odd?" asked Meredith.

Edward and Mira looked at each other, saying almost in unison

"Doesn't smell like snack food."

"That's disgusting," her mother said. "Though I suppose you may be well placed to judge such things." She looked contemplative. "If I don't smell . . . human then what do I smell like?"

"Rather like some of the children of the old ones, and a little like a Poukha," he said thoughtfully. "Though, I do not know how that could be."

"On that note, I'm definitely making tea. Anyone want some?" her mother asked.

"Always!" Mira exclaimed..

"So, Edward..." her mother continued when she returned with the tea tray. "How is it that you are supposed to help, exactly?"

"I promised Argent that I would back any play Mira wished to make regarding her inheritance."

"That has a rather broad scope to it," Meredith said.

"It has the benefit of being complete, without being prescriptive," he replied. This was the first time Mira had heard the actual wording of the promise he'd made Gran. It made sense of his behavior so far. It would wait to be seen how active he would become in protecting her interests, especially once the politics got more intense.

"And the inheritance?" Meredith asked. "What trouble is that likely to bring with it?"

"That rather depends on what Mira learned from her father," he said. "Though the Rede of Trees is a rather important artifact. It is revered by most of the races of Others, and by scholars and mages in more than one realm of reality."

"You said Gran had called me the custodian of the Rede?" asked Mira. "However, you also said I was a candidate for custodian?"

"It is said that the Rede chooses its own custodian, " he responded, "and also that only the current custodian can choose to pass it on. More than that is not really known. Neither Argent, nor the previous keeper talked about that aspect of things." He paused in thought. "I do know that the Rede cannot be seized unwillingly. It must have some ability to hide itself from the wrong candidates."

~~~

Terrific. So I have an unquiet book with an opinion of its own about who it wants to bother." Mira kept with her habit of referring to the Rede as a book, just in case misdirection was still needed. It was almost second nature for her to hide the whole truth from those around her.

Sipping her tea, and tracing the pattern of a misdirection rune into the table top, Mira waited to see what her mother would make of that.

"It sounds like your time of evading your father's world is coming to an end, love," her mother stated. "I am sorry."

"Not your fault at all, mother." Mira said. "It is entirely on me for agreeing to be helpful."

"What did your father have to say?" Meredith asked.

"I went to talk to him about something else. However, he let me know that Gran has gifted me with rather a lot more than the Rede." She looked over at Edward "So, backing my play is likely to become somewhat more complicated for you, as well."

"Oh? And what is the rest of the so-called gift?" Edward asked.

"Gran set things in motion in case she was away for more than five years" said Mira. "She designated her Council position to me, with all its proxies and assigns, effective at the Equinox in a couple of weeks."

Edward frowned. "That's going to mean having to show up for Council. It it will not be possible to avoid Justin," he glanced over at her mother, "Argent's assistant."

"Were you avoiding him, love?" Meredith asked.

"He seems to be interested in the Rede," Mira said. "And I'm not entirely sure it is a welcome interest."

"Are you thinking about taking up the Council position?" Meredith asked. "Is that entirely wise?"

"I am not sure there is a better option," said Mira. "There is apparently a vote coming up that will need some consideration. There are various factions arguing for the pros and cons of coming out to the human world." Mira threw her hands up in the air. "Some decision needs to be made, and I find I do care about how that vote plays out."

Mira was pleased her mother was taking an interest. While she spent most of her time ignoring the world, that didn't mean she lacked a keen grasp of events. She had originally become aware of the Others when she became involved with Mira's father. Now, it looked like their attraction may have been more like-to-like, rather than the Other-Human pairing Mira had always considered it to be. She thought the Dragon must be mistaken about the Poukha aspect of things, though she could see her mother as a descendent of the creative forces that made the world. Mira wasn't too sure how she felt about the shift that made in her own self-image. Her mother, though, seemed to take it in stride.

"Edward, how do you feel about how the Council position changes things?" Mira asked. It was more than time to start getting his active opinion.

"I cannot say it is expected, though the promise is still in effect," he claimed. "I have come to know you in the past few days. I would also not like to see you at Council without more than me to back you up, and having a position gives you authority. I think Argent planned as well as she could, given the circumstances."

"I wonder how she knew she would be gone for five years. She ought to be able to wish herself another body in that long."

"It took me most of five years to make an adequate form," he said.

"Yes, but she is wishborn. It takes her no time at all to manifest her wishes in the world."

"We have to assume that she has her reasons. The reasons of a star, though, may not be those of the rest of us."

"Father seemed to think there was more to my inheritance. Whatever it was, he wanted the family's interests to be represented."

"He's always been interested in pursuing power, by whatever means," said Meredith. "He cannot help himself."

"The Unseelie Court is also involved." Mira said. "They are calling home their wanderers. We learned that even the nobility has been called to Court.""

"That sounds like we should look for other movements among the Others," Edward said. "The Council meeting could become rather contentious."

"Perhaps we should head for Gran's rooms at the Enclave." Mira considered out loud. "It might be good to settle things with Justin, or at least get a sense of where he stands. Gran may also have left instructions for me?"

"I agree," Edward said. "It may also be good to know, in advance, what factions are allied."

"Mira, you will be careful, won't you?" requested her mother. "Stay tonight, and think things through before you leave."

"Yes, mum." Mira said. "I also have some thinking to do before we go anywhere. Edward, are you okay with staying until tomorrow?"

"Yes, that sounds like a good idea."

"Miranda, I have something I want you to take with you," her mother said. "I made a small piece of sculpture that I'd like you to have. I can fit it onto a necklace."

That was unusual. And a first for her mother to be making Mira jewelry. "Sure, it would be great to have something crafted by you. It would be a comfort."

"That's settled then. Make some more tea, will you dear?" her mother asked. "I'll go get the carving."

When her mother left the room, Mira put her hands on her hips, looking at Edward. "You and I are going to have to come to an understanding. I need to know what kind of support I can expect from you."

"Granted," he said. "I have been less than forthcoming."

"You don't say," Mira said, smiling to take the sting out of her words.

"I noticed that your paternal family tries to bind you with magic," he ventured "yet none of it seems to stick to you."

"Hmmm. Well, I like to do my own thing."

"I can see that," he said. "Does that same ability extend to people outside of your family?"

"It seems to work that way," she said. "Gran said my magic worked in a similar way to her own, that my wishing was particularly strong." She frowned in deep thought. "It looks like I may have that ability from more than one place, if what you said about my mother being Other was accurate.""

"My senses are very keen," he said "even in this rather limited form."

"I wonder what I get from my mother's side of the family?" she mused, "I certainly didn't get their creativity. Almost everyone in her Family is an Artist. Yes, with the capital 'A'."

Just then her mother came back into the room with a palm-sized wooden carving in her hands. "This was something I was playing with recently" she explained. Putting the carving into Mira's hands, she gestured at the entwined organic form. It looked a bit like runes or letters, when looked at in one way, yet it looked like a stylized, feathered serpent or phoenix, when looked at from the other side.

"It is beautiful." Mira said. "Thank you."

"It reminds me of you in some way", said her mother. "It is not entirely one thing or another, but is entirely its own thing, complete and unique."

Mira felt her eyes tear up. It was one of the nicest things her mother had ever said to her. It was a validation of the differences that made her who she was.

"Here, let me put that on a chain," Meredith said, producing a hand-made copper and bronze chain threaded with flat tapered bronze beads. Reaching for some pliers on a nearby shelf and a spool of wire, she quickly twisted a clasp around a convenient curve of the sculpture to secure it in place. "There, that should hold it. Wear it in good health."

"I am delighted. It reminds me of your paintings," Mira said. "All energy and motion, married together in a harmonious form.""

Her mother just smiled at her "Just like you, love, just like you."

28

RITUALS

After supper, they sorted themselves for sleep. Mira had her own room, of course. They fixed up the guest room at the far end of the upstairs hallway for Edward.

"Good night everyone," Meredith called from the bottom of the stairs. Mira thought it likely that she would do more painting before going to sleep. That would follow her pattern from when Mira was growing up.

Mira moved around her room, touching keepsakes and doing some thinking over the evening's conversations. She felt like her head was full of thoughts, thoughts that were jumbled and tangled like a basket of yarn. The decisions she would need to make weighed on her. She may need to give up the library in Seattle. Where would she live if she took up the Council position? Gran's rooms? When would she move? Would she move? Darn. Dr. Horrible, her ferocious Persian cat, hated moving. He'd certainly let her know about it. Would he be okay around Others? Would they want to eat him? She'd like to see them try it – they'd get a face full of fangs and claws that was for sure.

Mira paced back and forth across the cozy thick rug, her bare feet digging into the nubby pile. It was older than she was, but still holding up well. She was restless and felt like action needed to be taken, but no action could be taken just yet. She picked up a book, put it down again, checked her over-sized shoulder bag, said a gentle hello to the special books she'd tucked into a side pocket. She felt a little guilty letting the Dragon—Edward, she reminded herself—letting Edward think that one of those books was the Rede. It had been surprisingly easy to deflect that piece of information away, almost like the Rede itself didn't want to be discovered by anyone else.

? she heard the start of a question

??? It questioned again.

Be still she said. *I am thinking about you, not to you.*

The Rede's voice was coming through to her more clearly all the time. It freaked her out a bit that she didn't find that more disturbing.

I am here it conveyed, wistfully.

I am about to sleep. Be well. she sent back. She got a rumbly, sleepy slide of thoughts back, something about it dreaming her, or her dreaming with it. She wasn't entirely sure what that last had been.

Mira settled into comfortable sleep bottoms and a short black, t-shirt that said "BITE ME!" on the front in big white letters. It suited her mood for the present. Soon enough, the night time rituals of arranging the pillows in a boomerang shape, smoothing the covers, and settling down underneath them took away consciousness. She slid into a deep, and blissfully dreamless sleep. Or at least they were quiet dreams that did not much disturb her slumber.

That made it particularly annoying when she was woken from slumber by a loud sharp sound from downstairs. Had the kitten knocked over something big in the kitchen? Was someone trying to break in?

29

NIGHT NOISES

She grabbed a dressing gown, pulling on sheepskin boots, and tumbled outside, running into Edward heading downstairs at the same time.

"What?" she mumbled

"Don't know," he whispered. "Stay behind me."

They headed down the stairs quietly but quickly, only to see the backdoor closing as they reached the kitchen.

"After them!" she yelled, looking around the dining room. Several chairs had been pulled over, the tea tray was on the floor, and the kitten was hissing in the corner, fur standing on end, thoroughly wet from the cold, spilled tea. As Mira looked around the room, she noticed her backpack was missing, as well as her coat that had been slung over the back of the couch.

Edward came back in, looking disgruntled.

"Missed them."

"How many?" she asked.

"Two male figures, one tall and one medium height. They disappeared, not far down the road. I could not catch up with them in this form."

"Darn it! They got my backpack," said Mira

"Oh no! Did they get the Rede?"

"No, don't be silly. It isn't in my backpack," she said absently, picking up a chair to get to the tea tray. "Okay, the teapot is okay, but this cup has had it. Fetch me the broom over there will you?" she continued to clean up the contents of the tray. The kitten kept alternately hissing, and making mewling sounds. Poor confused beastie.

"Thanks." She swept the fallen sugar into a pile and dumped it into the garbage. "But they got my coat as well, and I loved that thing."

Edward picked up the other chairs and straightened the room. He took a closer look at the door.

"This lock has been forced," he said. "Why are there no wards on this place? Or even an alarm?"

"That wouldn't do much good. Mother would forget to arm the alarm—we tried that—and she is an Artist. The only locks she has are on her storage unit in the garage, and that's only locked when she's got a load of stuff ready for an art show. The insurance company insists. Are you sure they're gone?"

"Yes. I am so sorry I could not reach them before they disappeared."

"It looks like they were after the Rede, rather than the Art," Mira said, miserably. "Edward, this responsibility is beginning to get really complicated." Mira ran her hands through her sleep-tangled hair.

"I need some tea." The ritual actions of making tea, calmed her. Actively cleaning away the signs of intruders helped even more. She felt sick that her mother's world had been invaded by her troubles.

"The only ones who knew where I was going were my family..."

"I was coming to the same conclusion," he said, regret coloring his voice.

Mira yawned. "Maybe hot cocoa would be better. I'm going to set a chair under the door handle."

"I will stay down here for the remainder of the night." Edward insisted. "I feel terrible that I did not think to stand guard."

Mira mixed him a cocoa, and served herself a cup of milk laced with honey for the shock.

"That would be welcome, thank you." She picked up the kitten, who immediately started a rumbling purr that was an improvement on the hissing and crying, and then put him down on Edward's chest, where he curled up happily. "I'm going to head back to bed and see if I can get some more shut-eye."

"That sounds good. I will come get you in the morning."

Mira trudged up the stairs with her milk, feeling quite unsettled. If only her family knew she was coming here, then one of them must be responsible for their unwelcome night visitors. Breaking in to steal her backpack meant things were escalating. She wondered if someone thought they could make an easy grab for the Rede, not understanding its nature. It was pretty clear to her that Gran had played her hand close to her chest on this one as no-one but Mira seemed to know what, and where, the Rede was currently being held.

She would miss the contents of that particular bug-out backpack, but they were mostly clothes and comforts, and could be replaced. The biggest regret was some of her favorite jewelry, though none of that was expensive. Her most important stuff was in her oversized satchel-messenger bag, which she checked on as soon as she returned to her bedroom. It was still safe, with the books tucked into the side pocket, carefully zipped.

There had been one book in the bug-out bag, a grimoire that had lived there for some years. It had a sturdy leather cover and it was closed with a clever bit of magic, but the book was essentially harmless. She and Gran used to refer to it as *Baby's First Grimoire*. Mira kept it more for sentimental value than anything else. If someone managed to get it open, all they would find was thirteenth century arcana, annotated in invisible ink. She laughed a bit at the memory of invisible ink; that belonged to her pretentious phase when she was about twelve years old. She was sad to lose the little grimoire. It came from a period of time with a lot of happy memories. However, it may fool someone into thinking it to be the Rede, at least until it got passed along to someone who knew better.

This room could be warded, and she promptly did so, something she had not felt the need to do at her mother's place for years. She cast a basic charm on the door, something to keep everyone away except for her mother and Edward. Maybe she would be able to get some more sleep, before dealing with events in the morning. Tomorrow looked like it was going to be a busy day, and she would need what rest she could get.

30

UNEXPECTED GIFTS

Mira woke to the sound of birds some hours later. This close to the forest she could hear the sound of a faux jay, one of the big blue ones, making a racket, in amongst the calling of crows. If the crows and jays were about making their usual morning rounds of conversation, no predators, human or otherwise were about. It was only when they got quiet that there was cause for alarm.

The sun slanted through the window in a diffuse pattern of light, catching on the various crystals she'd hung one lazy summer, years ago now. The light refracted around the room. Mira lay there enjoying the comfort of the familiar. Soon enough, the day would bring its own challenges. For this moment, she would stretch and center. She considered whether the Martial Way would serve her well enough for now. It would access protective magic that she'd put aside while living in the city, but did not demand as much energy as the more active Warrior Path. She had the Warrior Path in reserve, should events require it. Without invoking it yet, she took the first few mental steps to access the runes she had spent so long putting into place. If she needed it, it was keyed to be available to her with a word and a touch. This part of her training is part of what had allowed her to stay hidden for so long, and this particular technique was one Gran had used herself during her long life. She said it had been useful to her over her long years. With it, Mira could key states that brought different abilities to the fore. She could also hide those abilities by changing states.

? The Rede appeared to be curious whenever she shuffled her internal states. *Becoming?* it questioned.

Not quite yet she replied. There was a sudden kaleidoscope of images whirling through her mental landscape. A glowing rune spun into being, insistently presented on a mental screen. It was not one she had seen before, and seemed to be offered by the Rede.

For me? Mira asked. *What will it do?* she asked. If it was a gift, she had, at least, become wary enough to ask what new impact it would have on her. A feeling of warmth, light and sound cascaded through her, along with words in a musical language Mira was almost familiar with.

Strength she felt and heard. That sounded like something useful, she mused.

Done she heard, and was swept up into a blurring of sensory experiences.

Mira felt her mind and body stretched and overwhelmed with sensation. A kaleidoscope of visual and aural sensations, scents, abrupt nerve and muscle twitches followed. She breathed through it, waiting for the impact to abate.

Damn it, that hurt. she exclaimed, when she could catch her breath again. *What did you do?*

More of the Now it said, in its cryptic way. *Stronger*.

As Mira turned her head, she saw streamers in the corners of her eyes. It felt like her sight had been shifted into overdrive. She could *see* an overlay of possibilities on every object in the room. Closing her eyes, she invoked the rune that muted her *sight*, making it easier to move in the world. Opening her eyes again, she expected the room to return to normal. However, it appeared that was not going to happen easily.

The Rede had done this. It had amplified her Sight to a degree where she could not easily turn it off. This was going to take some work.

!!! Mira asserted. *I need to be able to turn this off.* Then hastily added *When I wish*.

There was a feeling of confusion for a moment, followed by the presentation of another big glowing rune. It appeared to be related to the first one, but was a different color.

Is this one going to hurt too?

She got a feeling of apology, and a sense of waiting.

Okay, go for it Mira was not surprised to feel another cascade of shifts inside her, changing things around, a feeling of the Rede rummaging in her head for concepts and connections, and rearranging what it found there. It was the oddest feeling and quite painful, but she gritted her teeth until it was over, being ready for it this time.

When it was done, everything felt a little muted and far away.

??? Mira felt from the Rede. Mira guessed that was questioning whether that's what she wanted. She visualized the first rune, got a small spike of pain behind her eyes, and an intensity of the Sight that brought with it an amplification of the rest of her senses, hearing, kinesthetic feeling, a rush of scent and perception. She settled with that for a moment, feeling a little nauseous from the bombardment of her senses. Applying discipline, she centered herself, balancing her inner energies. That seemed to bring things more into alignment, though everything was still too loud.

Okay, here goes she said, and visualized the second symbol. This time, the pain was a little less, as if there was space now in her head for the rune to express. The feeling of intensity backed off a little. Sound became more muted. The light became less bright. And the birds only sounded as normally loud as they were on any other morning. Mira liked knowing she could control her magic, and though this was a new level of intensity, she wanted to practice with it. Bracing herself for the expected pain, she invoked the first rune again. This time, the pain was fleeting, and almost bearable. When she invoked the second rune, there was no pain this time. Good, this was working. Mira rapidly cycled between the runes, getting accustomed to the new sensory experiences. When they were firmly under her control, she felt exhausted, but triumphant.

It was clear, though, that she would have to think more quietly around the Rede. The strength it offered was not without a learning curve, and like all magic it had a price. She could sense the Rede more distinctly now. It had a green scent like moss and the wild woods, and a sound like the echo in deep, underground caverns. The sun had changed angle by the time she finished, moving along past dawn. It was time to grab a shower and make some tea, followed by breakfast.

When Mira bounced out of bed, she nearly stumbled. Her physical reflexes also seemed to be impacted, muscles responding more quickly to the signals from her brain. This was familiar to her from the Warrior Path, but, she checked inside, she had not invoked that yet. This must be another side effect of the strength runes.

Stronger she heard, along with a mélange of impressions that said satisfaction. Mira would need to be careful as she assimilated the changes that had not quite steadied into her physical body.

31

BALANCING STRENGTH

Showering was a whole new experience. Her skin was so sensitive that the water running over it sent eddies of whole-body pleasure through her, in ripples of sensation. Every nerve ending was alive. The muscles felt smooth and strong like oiled springs. She shuddered with pleasure, enjoying the simple task of cleansing her body far more than she really ought to indulge in for this long. Harmless enough, though it reminded her that it had been a while since she'd caught up with her good friend Ken, a friendly partner, and rather an excellent lover. She wondered if she would be able to take up that part of her life again. The life she had built was satisfying and comfortable in a way that she appreciated. It would be good to keep what she could of it.

She indulged herself in another few minutes of drenching herself in the hot flowing water, washing her hair as well. Stepping out of the shower, it only took her a few minutes to dry off and braid her hair. Picking clothes from the dresser took only a few minutes. She chose soft pants with a microfiber tank and a draped tunic-vest in a mossy green. The color was a good match for both her mood and the energy of the Rede.

She met Edward in the kitchen, already making tea.

"Blessings on the tea maker," she called softly.

"There you are" he said, pouring her a mug of tea. It was one of her favorite cups, thin porcelain with a slight outward curve at the lip. She took a sip, savoring the Darjeeling blend. "You look rested."

"I am feeling well," she said, realizing at that moment that she felt marvelous. "Has mother appeared yet?"

"Yes, a little while ago," he said "but she only wanted tea."

"Did you let her know about the break in?" Mira asked. He gestured at the chair propped against the door.

"She noticed, but seemed preoccupied." He shrugged. "She seemed anxious to get back to her work, once she was certain we were both okay and that none of the Art had been touched."

Mira laughed out loud, throwing back her head in delight.

"That's my mother," she said with a sigh. "Okay then, let's be practical. I'll make breakfast, and then we can decide if we head for my apartment, back to the family to confront them about the break in, or directly for Gran's rooms and the Council. Your choice," she said airily, waving her hands in a swift circle in the air.

Scrambled eggs seemed the quickest thing. She put those on, started toast, and grated some cheese from a big block of cheddar. Slicing tomatoes, she arranged them on two plates, taking out a third shallow bowl to put in the oven for her mother to eat later. Mira buttered the toast, put out marmalade to go with it, and served up the eggs with the cheese. Cheesy eggs was one of her go-to meals, comforting and familiar. She felt the energy coursing through her body, making a delight of the simplest actions. She felt a bit like a child again, easily distracted by the glow of the world.

The kitten curled around her ankles, pouncing at her toes and mock growling as a way to get her attention. She glanced sideways at Edward, to see how he would react, and shared a small spoonful of eggs with the tiny feline. The treat of human food was enough to quieten his meows as he dug into the small serving. Edward looked as if feeding kittens was a perfectly normal activity. Good. At least he didn't seem to feel like cats were snacks. It would distress her mother, and not amuse the cat goddess, Bast. Her mother kept a shrine to Bast in the entry way, and gave it regular attention if the fur pillow and incense were a sign of devotional activity.

"So?" she ventured, finishing up her last bite of eggs. "Thoughts about our next steps?"

"Was there anything in the bag that is irreplaceable?" he asked first. "Or can you put together another bag here?"

"I have a pack in the downstairs closet, so we're good to go," she said. "Gran favored being prepared". She strode over to the closet, rummaged around behind boots, last year's winter coats, and some miscellaneous garden supplies. "Yes, it's still here." Mira hauled out the backpack. It was just about the same size and make as the last one, only this one was purple instead of brown. She unzipped a couple of pockets to check it. "Everything I need is here."

Edward looked bemused by the appearance of the fully packed kit. "How many of those do you have?" he asked.

"Oh, about six I think," she replied absently. "I have them stashed here and there. Wherever I might need to bug out to, or from."

"You are full of surprises," he stated. "I thought only Dragons planned for every eventuality."

"You have no idea," she said wryly. "Gran used to run drills when I was a kid. I guess I just kept it up. Makes me feel close to her, now that she's gone."

"That makes our decisions simpler. Do you have something suitable for a Council session in there?"

"I have a dress that'd do in a pinch, though I have more formal clothes in Gran's rooms, if we're going there. I'd prefer those. It wouldn't do to make a bad impression."

"How long has it been since you lived at the Residence?" Edward asked.

"More than eight years since I lived there full time. I went off to study at the University of Washington." She returned the plates to the kitchen and rinsed them.

"You realize everyone is going to think I'm the same precocious child Gran dragged with her everywhere?" Mira said.

"I think they will be desperately surprised should they attempt to dismiss you as only a child," he stated. "Though you are," he said delicately "very young. Only in the first childhood of that body."

"Ah, but I am older than you are in yours," she said with some humor. "Even though you are a very venerable Dragon, with aeons of experience in your Other form."

He laughed with her, clearly willing to accept her view of his newness in his current body.

"It is all a matter of perspective," he affirmed. "I can always change form if we need to impress people with the gravitas of having a Dragon call you friend."

"Now that I would pay good money to see."

He managed to look both proud and bashful, a peculiar look on his youthful face. Whatever he'd contrived when creating his human form, it did not seem he would be growing a beard any time soon. His face remained as free of morning stubble as it had been for the past few days. His whole look was at seeming odds with the true being she sensed him to be. As a first human form, which it was clear this was, it was good craft. He did seem to be getting more comfortable in it all the time.

Mira thought she would have to watch her habit of treating him like a younger relative, as that may lead to her thinking him as harmless as his mild human-looking form invited. She knew better than that, especially given her own experience with slight-of-hand and misdirection. Treating him as harmless? That would be a mistake.

32

CHOICES

D id you think about the choices I outlined last night?" she enquired.

"Yes. It seems that heading for your Gran's chambers to see what formal instructions she may have left for the Council position," he tilted his head to one side to gauge her reaction "may be prudent."

"I agree. Let me say goodbye here, and we can leave." Mira headed for her mother's studio.

"Mum?" she called at the open doorway. She could just see her mother to the side of an enormous canvas. She had a paint brush, thankfully clean, pushed through her hair to keep it out of the way. The early morning light limned her with a golden glow. Mira's heart ached. Her mother was so beautiful. She was perfectly balanced, centered in the light, and intent on the canvas in front of her. "Mother?" she called again, gently.

It took a few minutes before she noticed Mira's voice. Mira waited patiently for the sound to filter through to her, being no stranger to her parent's keen focus on the creative. Meredith blinked rapidly, looking around, having finally noticed her call. "You called?" she asked, wiping her hands on a paint rag. She put her brush into a jar of turpentine, wiped her hands again on a cleaner rag, and headed across the studio to Mira.

"Is the Work going well?" Mira asked.

"I need to think about what comes next. It looks like I'll be here for most of the day" said Meredith. "Best break for breakfast, or I'll be interrupted by my belly aching later."

"We're going to head out shortly," said Mira.

"I'm sorry there was trouble last night. You didn't lose anything important did you?"

"There was that old Grimoire in there, and I'm bummed about the coat. It was comfortable," she grumbled. "But I'm the one who's sorry. Sorry I brought trouble to your doorstep."

"Oh honey, don't worry about it," Meredith said. "I'll let you ward the house against ill intent before you go, if it will make you feel better?"

"Really? I'd love to." Her mother had always shrugged off her suggestions to ward the place. It was quite a concession for her to ask for Mira to do it now. It was also an indication that she was not nearly as blasé about the break-in as she appeared.

33

HOUSE BLESSING

Mira regarded the Dragon ruefully, wondering if he would be interested in helping her ward the house. It was said Dragon magic was particularly good at wards that stood the test of time. She wanted something flexible enough to accommodate her mother's absentmindedness, yet strong enough to keep out the kind of troublemakers who had wandered in last night. She would need something that the house brownie would feel comfortable with as well. Mira thought a variation of the methods she used in the human world, together with some Dragon magic, might make a good blend.

"Edward?" she queried. "How would you feel about helping me to ward the house for my mother?"

"Hmmm?" he responded absently, being caught in perusing one of Meredith's vivid paintings. This time the painting was of a wind storm at the edge of a forest, the balance of light and darkness at the point of tilting towards darkness, but not quite there yet. Driving slashes of wind and rain bent the tree branches. A small figure, mostly a suggestion of a hooded shape than something figurative, was right at the hinge between the field and the tree line, the angle of the form suggesting struggle against the wind. The small form seemed to be almost at the trees, yet the painting seemed to suggest the trees might be more trouble than the storm.

"Edward? When you have a moment..." Mira shrugged and went to make another cup of tea. She was more than experienced with people getting lost in paintings. Sooner or later he would realize she needed his attention. In the meantime, she was going to rummage in some closets and see if she could find some supplies to use in warding the house. She wanted to find the glass beads florists sometimes used for decorative accent. Her mother sometimes liked to add small smashed pieces of glass to her paintings. The florist beads were flat on one side and glued well to a canvas. Mira would use them for her own purposes, putting the beads over doors and windows to anchor the energies of the house wards. Unless Edward had a better idea.

Mira found the beads, along with some bags of colored sand. Those may be interesting for use when they warded the outside of the house. When Mira warded an apartment, she could use salt at the edge of the sacred space she was creating, however, here salt would endanger the garden. Sand would be a much better alternative; also she liked the small pieces of mica glinting in the sand. Sometimes, when working magic, the elements she used were more because of the emotional resonance they had for her. Sure, she could make up a reason that satisfied her intellect later, but the real reasons she chose certain ingredients were often more linked to her intuition. It maddened a chum of hers who practiced human ceremonial magic; he always wanted the magical correspondences and ingredients to be predictable. Mira laughed. Life was, she found, much more organic than that. She put both the glass beads and the bags of sand on the table and settled to drink her tea. Assam this time, with honey and lemon.

"Mira? Did you need something?" Edward asked in due time.

"Yes, but it is not urgent. I could wait on your enjoyment of the painting."

"The quality of the light, the composition..." Edward gazed over his shoulder at the painting again and sighed happily. "So, what can I assist you with?"

"I am going to ward the house for my mother. I wondered if you might like to help?"

"I would be honored," he said. "What do you have in mind?"

"Using the laws of similarity and contagion," she responded. "I am thinking of using some stones, or rather glass beads to act as a common element to bind together the different energies of the Working."

"You might also use the structure of the house, its bones, and the windows," he suggested.

"Yes, that as well. Though for me using a common or similar material makes it easier for me to focus and concentrate my energies. Then I put the stones over the doors and windows, and at the various entry places into the house," she continued.

"Good sound practice," he agreed. "Why glass in particular?"

"For me, it seems to partake of all the elements. It is formed of earth, created in fire..."

"Cooled in air, and yet remains a slow liquid?" he finished.

"Yes exactly." Mira agreed. She thought of old glass in windows becoming gradually thicker at the bottom, the liquid aspect of the material acting according to its nature.

"And therefore ready to take a charge and become a matrix of energy that holds the Working in place?" he asked.

He reached out for the glass beads, holding them in his elegant hands. He was clearly sensing the latent energies of the raw materials.

"These are somewhat similar, though I can tell they come from different batches of glass. Will that matter for you? I rather like the thought of more similarity. Though, as you said, putting them together for a first charge, and then doing more when they are separated may be all right. They are similar enough."

"Do you have another idea? I do not mind using a pure energy working," Mira said.

"Not at all. These would be fine. I wonder, though, if you might have a bucket of rocks or sand?"

"Sand? Certainly. Those five pound bags have sand in them."

"Let me see what I might contrive?" he asked.

Mira made a 'go ahead' gesture, interested to see what he might do. Dragons were masters of the elements. He would have a keen sense of the earth beneath the house, right down through the bedrock and into the molten core of the world. When he opened his senses, he would be able to feel the surrounding rocks, the deep water under the ground, and even the range of mountains far to the east. He would feel the Pacific from here to the coast of Australia if he chose to indwell his consciousness in the strata of the earth. What he would make of a bag of sand or rock, she was ready to learn.

As he reached for the bags of sand, sweeping three of them into his hands at the same time, she sensed his energy shifting more into the aether and the Between. While she was aware much of a Dragon existed in that liminal space between worlds, she hadn't really thought about where he put the rest of him while he was being human. The human form was clearly much smaller than the size he was accustomed to being.

Perhaps the energy that made a Dragon able to exist, impossibly, in the world, came from that place. Certainly that made sense of things Gran had said to her years ago. It almost seemed she had been preparing Mira to deal with Dragons. Mira used the rune for sight to see more deeply into the world of form. What she saw there surprised and delighted her. His Dragon form was like the firstborn of the world. He appeared to her as a bronze and black Earth Dragon, the bronze color that of the deep earth and the black glittering with the sparkle of void and stars.

"There!" he exclaimed. The bags around the sand disappeared in a contained burst of heat. In front of him on the table was a glittering pile of crystalline, clear glass rounds, about the size of her smallest fingernail. "Much more similar."

Mira couldn't help herself. She clapped her hands together and grinned at him like a small child.

"Wow!" she exclaimed. She reached out and carefully picked up a couple of the glass beads. The heat had been tidily removed, leaving a polish on the glass beads that glittered. The edges were perfectly smooth, though the inside of the beads fractured light into a rainbow of colors.

"Will those do?" he asked.

"Do?" she asked. "Why yes, I think these will be perfect." She could have made the other glass beads work for her purposes, but given the option of using Dragon-formed glass, that was clearly superior. She took pause to be aware of how much power resided in the seeming of a feckless young man. The casual way he shifted the sand into glass had the power of lightning and storm that shifted in his eyes. Eyes that were, at present, a gleaming gold.

"Where would you like these?" he asked.

"I thought I might make use of your greater height to put these over the doors, windows, at every entry way into the house?"

He made a gesture towards the beautiful glass. Most of it swirled up into the air, whirling between his palms. It glittered in the sunlight.

"Did you want to add your energy to the materials?" he asked politely.

"If you do not mind holding the stones in place?" she asked.

"With pleasure," he said, grinning. His hair had fallen down over his face, lending him an anime character look to go along with the casual way he kept the whirling glass in the air.

Mira concentrated on the elements of the spell. Safety, protection, comfortable homecoming, allowing inspiration and creativity to flourish, keeping away unwelcome visitors and distractions, allowing positive energy to enter in. When she had the separate pieces built upon each other into a single composite form, she gently pushed the form into the center of the energy between Edward's hands. Then she let it go.

The mass glowed more brightly for a moment and seemed to pulse.

Edward nodded to her and pushed his hands closer together for a moment, then widened his arms. The glass beads swirled around the room, missing the people and paintings but landing in deliberate places. Mira saw several alight over windows and doors as she watched the pattern in her head spread out around the house.

"Or you could do it like that," she said approvingly. "Will they stay in place?"

"Yes. I made them melt for a moment on contact, so the stones will not need glue."

"Brilliant!" Mira said. "Elmer's glue or crazy glue are great, but it takes me ages to get it off myself afterwards."

She reached out to sense the matrix of energy around the house. She could feel that there were small glass beads around the outside walls, at the edges of the foundation, along the driveway, and around the outer buildings. She could feel tiny microscopic dots of rounded glass around the pipes and electrical conduits into the house. There were even glass beads around the chimney flue and along the wastewater drains. She could also feel the ones near the washer and dryer vents. Quite a satisfactorily complete job, and in no time at all. She could get accustomed to this level of 'help'.

"Would you like me to anchor it to the bedrock?" Edward asked. "It would keep the warding fueled without any further need for attention."

"Really? Could you? It would make me feel so much better about mom's safety."

"Consider it done." His energy brightened and darkened into shadow again for a moment. He nodded, then spread his hands to say that the task was complete.

Mira could feel the energy of the Working stabilize and become smooth. She could sense that with each pulse of energy, the spell was renewed, drawing energy from deep in the earth.

"Thank you, friend." Mira said. "I learn much in your company."

"I am happy to help keep such a brilliant artist safe from harm," he replied. "Shall we think about continuing our journey?"

"I think our work here is done," Mira replied.

She had learned much more about his nature by sharing the magical work with him. That he was an Earth Dragon and a Star Dragon at the same time; that he was generous with his energy; and that he was grounded in time in a way she had not seen in anyone other than Gran. It bore thinking on. She did not think she would be underestimating him again anytime soon.

34

A POCKET FULL OF PORTALS

'm ready to go." Mira said, tipping a couple of glass beads that matched the ones they had used when they warded the house into a small pouch, adding it to the ones she had collected at the places they had visited over the past few days. Keeping a couple of the beads with her would enable her to check in on the house from a distance, and to return here along the inner paths at need.

The small pile of beads they had not used she left in a bowl with a note for her mother to enjoy. Perhaps they would even end up in some paintings. These were beads that had not been part of the house warding, but were indeed Dragon Glass. Mira would be interested to see what impact the stones had when mixed into one of her mother's creative projects.

A pocket full of places, she thought, tucking the leather pouch into her front pocket. "Do you have a good anchor for the Residence?" She was referring to the chateau that contained chambers for the resident Council members. It sat in landscaped grounds with a variety of habitats, terraced into the sacred mountain, with both formal and informal meeting places.

"I usually prefer to transit at one of the established Gates" he said. "However, if you prefer to arrive without attention, I do have an alternate location I can use."

"If we're going to be noticed, perhaps it is best to arrive by the usual means. If we arrive without giving notice, someone is bound to make an issue of it."

"I agree. The Terrace Gate, then, is my recommendation"

"I agree." She shrugged on her purple backpack and put her big shoulder bag on her left shoulder. Edward reached out his left hand. Mira centered and shielded, taking his left hand with her right. He nodded, and they transited.

This time, the chronons spiraled around her, scattering possibilities that seemed more coherent and tangible. She reached internally for a couple of the lines that appeared, braiding them together deliberately. She would take charge of time.

Yes she heard the Rede murmur inside.

The colors were suddenly brighter, striving to become, as they travelled through the lines, passing through the intersection of the vision she had just touched with her thoughts.

35

THE TERRACE GATE

The Terrace Gate was a fixed location, with stone-carved pillars and symbols incised in gold, bronze and magic. The lintel at the top was thick with runes and sigils; the magic of the Gate made it an effortless transit place from anywhere in the Seven Realms. There were, she knew, many more than seven worlds, however, the Seven were those tied by alliance or treaty, as much as by affinity in space and time. Other worlds had different gates, and some places required multiple gates and journeys between to reach.

Mira and Edward arrived centered in the Gate, appearing in the middle of a circle inscribed into the granite. The transition created a silence for a moment. The potential of both spaces were balanced though in the moment of arrival they were present only in the Gate, not in either the place they came from, nor yet the place they had arrived. As the potential realized, sound and time gradually coalesced.

The quality of the light on the Mountain had a slightly violet hue, the light of a sun that was shifted a little in spectrum from that of the human world they had travelled from.

The weather here was always the same, pleasant and perfect, if a little predictable. Impossible birds sang in trees that were, on the Terrace, forever in spring foliage. Elsewhere in the grounds, the other seasons were represented, however here the apple blossoms were pale pink and white against the spiral-curved flagstones. The scent of the blossoms perfumed the air, accompanied by the scent of narcissus and jasmine along the path that appeared in front of them.

They walked between stone statues of Others in all their various natural forms, gryphons and satyrs, dragons and sirens, fae creatures from the light and dark courts, all the shapes of the People, including a ban sidhe and a vanara. The forms, though still and sculpted, seemed to watch them as they advanced across the terrace.

If she looked away, the statues seemed to move, but only when she was not looking directly at them. She could see small hints of motion from the corners of her eyes. They did not move from their places however, their poses seemed to shift slightly from moment to moment. These had the feeling of living statues imbued with energy.

Ahead of them were the smaller gates. From a stone gatehouse with a crenelated tower off to one side, watchers could see new arrivals crossing the terrace, affording a measure of security to the Council during times of War, the like of which had not been seen for a couple of millennia. The gatehouse did not appear to warrant watchers at present, and they passed it by with barely a glance. Certainly they received no challenge. Perhaps the statues were serving the function of the usual gate guardians, Mira thought. They seemed to be more aware and awake than she remembered them from when she was last here at this gate with Gran, nearly a decade ago.

36

THE RESIDENCE

As they approached the Residence, a tall woman approached them and bowed. She had the androgynous form of a bird shape shifter. Mira remembered her.

"Lady Sigourney," she returned the bow, acknowledging her greeting, adding an inclination of her head in respect for her station as Chatelaine of the Residence. "How gracious of you to greet us."

"It is a delight to see you here in our halls again. My condolences on your Grandmother's change of state," she said delicately. "Felicitations on your inheritance."

"Lady Sigourney," Edward bowed more shallowly, his bow signifying respect to a younger person. Mira could see that puzzled the Chatelaine, however, she was far too good mannered to allow her lack of recognition to slight a guest.

"I am here to visit my Grandmother's chambers" said Mira, deliberately not introducing Edward. Let her think of him what she willed for now. "For family matters. Not in any official capacity."

"Your privacy will be respected." Lady Sigourney would see to it that word spread of her arrival, and of her oblique request to be allowed time to visit without taking any official stance on her Gran's request to transfer her Council membership. "Please let me know if you require any assistance."

Mira nodded and bowed again, with gratitude. "Thank you for your kindness" she said. "I know my way, however, if we could trouble you to send someone with refreshments in a short time, it would be very welcome."

"Be assured that will be a minor task," said Lady Sigourney. "If it would suit you, please contact me with any other needs. Would it suit you to have hospitality provided this evening?"

Mira had a recollection that this was part of the usual practice. "I will contact you with further needs once I have assessed our situation."

"Very well," she smiled. Mira got the sense that she was doing okay, for a child, and was going to have some leeway before the grown-ups required anything of her. She guessed that from their vantage point, anyone under a thousand years old was a kid, though, so she didn't take it personally. It was an honor to have the Chatelaine greet her personally, rather than have one of her handmaidens do it for her. However, that was likely a gesture of respect for her Gran. She'd need to earn her own respect from here on.

Edward followed closely behind her, a step behind her left shoulder, in the position of an ally. Mira thought he may be overdoing it, as no danger had yet presented itself. Yet he was an old Dragon, so she would be guided by his sense of appropriate response to danger levels in the Residence. Gran cast a big shadow, and she had always felt the place to be fairly safe. That didn't mean it was safe now that Gran was gone. Mira was abruptly very grateful for Edward's presence at her back.

The corridors were longer than a reasonable person would expect. There was art, though not up to Mira's admittedly demanding standard, on the walls with mirrors, sculptures, and free-standing sentries both living and animated, along the way. She ignored them in favor of recalling the direct route to Gran's chambers. If she could think of the decorations as if they were part of a well-appointed high-end hotel, that would stop them from distracting her.

Most of the doors were also warded. She expected no different from her Gran's chambers. However, in this case, she had been keyed into the wards when she was a child, and should be able to come and go at will. At least she hoped she was still keyed in and that her energy signature had not changed too much in the intervening time. It would be a tad embarrassing to need to ask housekeeping for help in opening the door.

37

GRAN'S CHAMBERS

Fortunately, her hopes were realized. When she placed her palm against the middle of the door, it failed to bite her. The doors opened easily. Mira wondered for a moment what mechanism allowed Housekeeping to come and go, with their varied staff members, yet kept out the curious, or merely mischievous denizens of the Residence. Maybe something as simple as a fob on the inside of the suite that resonated with some token given to housekeeping. She would need to ask; likely she would be required to change the wards to her own custom configuration sometime soon.

The chambers were well aired, and had no feeling of being deserted. It was as if Gran had merely stepped away for a moment. Should she return some millennia, in some new body, her expectation would be to find her apartment ready for her use. The long lived had such a different perspective on places they claimed as their own. Mira had always thought of herself as one of the ephemerals, with a single life. That may no longer be entirely accurate, given what she was learning about both sides of her clan. However, a lifetime of habit was not changed overnight.

Closing the ornate doors behind them, she put her back-pack against the side wall and moved across the room to where she remembered Gran's study to be. Mira was surprised to find it also warded. The door required a firm pressure and a mental announcement before it yielded to her. The reason became clear – there was an envelope in the middle of the antique desk with Mira's full name Miranda Ambrose Astrum, inscribed on it in Gran's handwriting. There was no dust on the desk, nor on the envelope. That meant either that someone had delivered the envelope to this place, Gran had placed the room in stasis until Mira arrived, or the envelope may have been delivered from Gran, wherever she was, just this instant. In any case, it was impressive to find the missive waiting for her here.

"May I come in?" asked Edward, hesitating just outside the doorway.

"Certainly. There's even a Dragon-sized chair in here." Mira pointed to an enormous armchair, made of heavy wood, and padded with brocaded cushions.

"Yes, I remember it fondly," he responded, settling his tall lanky form into the giant-sized, or rather, dragon-sized chair. Just how big was the Dragon? No doubt she would find out at some stage.

"Great. There's a letter for me. Guess we'd better see what it has to say."

"Are you sure you want me here while you read it?" he asked.

"I don't see why not. You are the bearer of messages. It looks like this one has some other requirements around it though, timing being one of them. This must be one of many messages delivered from Gran."

Mira walked around behind the desk, put her shoulder bag on the corner of it, and put the backpack to one side. She settled into Gran's gorgeous tapestry chair. She broke the wax seal to open the letter. Mira took a deep breath, centered herself, and began to read. It was not long. It just put the current situation into perspective, asked Mira to take the Council seat, and apologized for the inconvenience. This must be the first apology she had ever heard of Gran providing, to anyone. She must have felt that events had spiraled out of her usually iron control. Gran let her know, in very few words, what she actions she would have taken were she present, but left it in Mira's hands to do as she wished. The word 'wished' was underlined, just to make sure she did not miss the point.

When she finished reading the short letter, Mira handed it across to Edward. She settled back into the chair, pulled up one leg, and wrapped her arms around it. She rested her chin on her raised knee, contemplating the changes wrought in her life in just a few short days. Yes, some of them had begun over five years ago when she agreed to look after the Rede. That didn't matter. Her dreams had been unquiet for months now. Gradually, the chronons bound up in the Rede were seeping into the groundwater of her being, changing her in ways that she could not begin to imagine. She had tried to look the other way, like a small child ignoring the figure in the closet. However, Mira had not started acting on the shifts that were occurring until Edward came stumbling in out of the storm. She felt like some part of that storm traveled with them, even now.

Edward took his time. He was quite deliberate as he carefully unfolded the vellum and read the handwriting.

"It is good to see Argent's hand again" he remarked. When he had reached the end of the missive, he looked up at Mira. "It is clear that in this, too, you have your Grandmother's trust. I can do no less." He bowed his head, and put the letter neatly back in the middle of the desk.

As he had been reading, Mira noticed a pressure building in the outer rooms, almost like the barometric pressure was shifting. She could hear a slight shift in the sounds, a humming that was slightly off key.

Was that another storm rising? Mira wondered as a crackle of light illuminated the room. A rumbling sound followed. Crack. More lightning. She thought the storm she'd been thinking of was metaphor, not something that would wander indoors complete with CGI special effects. What was this? A movie script? The light cracked again, blue, white and purple, breaking apart into particles like confetti.

Mira looked to the ward stone sitting on the desk. Nothing should be coming here from outside the wards. There was a scent of ozone in the air. Another rumble of thunder, the ward stone flickered in response and a hollow boom came from the outer chamber.

"Edward?" she sent him a startled glance.

He growled, a bass deep sound like the grinding of an earthquake.

"Wait!" he said.

She counted the sounds between the lightning and thunder. It seemed to be getting further apart. As a reflex, she centered, anchored herself to the ward stone and gathered her energies.

Wait came from within. For once, the Dragon and the Rede were in agreement.

Mira felt pressure building inside her. Behind her eyes burned. The rune for the Warrior Way presented itself as she blinked.

Now Mira made a complex hand gesture, and pressed both middle fingers to her forehead while subvocalizing the trigger word. The Warrior Way blossomed inside her. Weapons, complex spells she had readied in advance, were all accessible to her, including attack and defense forms.

Mira reached for and triggered a defense cloud, sending it to integrate with the wards Gran had left in place. She held ready another layer of defense caltrops, twisted charms to cripple any physical attackers, and sent out seeker spells. Mira held ready a chronon bomb, but would not use it unless pressed. It would rip attackers out of time.

Edward glowed, his human form overshadowed by a dragon-shaped cloak of scintillating might. Hands raised, head thrown back, he ROARED. His roar was deafening, layers of sound so intense she could see the sound waves in the visible spectrum. The waves of sound moved out, and where they moved, their vibrancy canceled the thunder. The sound shook the room even more than the attack coming from elsewhere. The intensity of the sound rocked Mira back on her heels, though she was braced and shielded.

Mira focused on neutralizing the light energy being aimed at the rooms. She reached for a magnetism spell that muted the lightning. It flickered and went out. The room was in darkness.

With a great booming sound, the outer door to the chambers vibrated with a sizzling rumble, and all sound abruptly ceased. Mira gestured, and the room was lit with mage fire, cold blue light in a nimbus around her hands.

"What?" she cried. Pressure she didn't know she had been feeling inside her head receded. The Dragon growled, deep in his chest.

"It is gone," he stated "For now."

38

MESSAGES

W hat was that?" she asked.

"Someone trying to end your possibilities," he said. "In common parlance, to kill you," he continued. "And me. Which was a mistake."

"Which part? Trying to kill me, or trying to kill you?"

"Yes."

"Who?"

"Now that's the question, isn't it?" He started pacing up and down in front of the desk. "Someone does not want you to be here." He slapped his hands against his thighs. "And they are foolish enough to stage an attack." Slap. Slap. "Here." Slap.

Mira sent the mage light up to rekindle the illumination of the study. Slap. Slap. A pause. Slap. He paced some more. Slap. Pace. Slap. Slap.

"Stop that!" she said, referring of course to him slapping his thighs. It was exceedingly annoying.

"If I change shape?"

"Don't. Not yet," Mira said.

Mira sent a pulse of energy to her seeker spell. It returned with a partial image that she would need to think about. Through the half-light, she could see a layered robe, dusty light through a high, slanted window, and she saw the image of a pale white hand holding a dark shadowed key.

She had a sense that she had missed a clue. Something to do with their arrival at the gate. It was nearly there, but she lost the train of thought. She hoped it would come back to her.

Mira glanced over towards Edward. She could see the outline of Edward's raith body, the subtle layer of auric body to the outside of the subtle body and inside the aura. It was still visible as a Shadow Dragon, though gradually the Dragon was shrinking in size, being absorbed into the human shadow as the threat moved further away from them. A rumbling sound came from deep inside him, reminding her of her Persian cat, Dr. Horrible, after a victorious brawl with a local raccoon.

She could feel her own aspect changing as well, the Warrior Path was still invoked. Mira said the word and touched the rune inside her, putting The Warrior Path back into dormant aspect. It was too costly in terms of energy to stay in that path longer than the battle required. It was there, and could be invoked again if needed, more quickly next time as it had already been triggered once. She took a deep breath, took the excess energy and sent it to cycle in a pattern in her auric field. Take it down a notch, she told herself. Mira firmly reached for the Martial Way, and centered. The Martial Way gave her access to defensive stances, but was not as demanding of internal or external energies.

"This is supposed to be neutral territory?" Mira questioned in an aggrieved tone.

"There appears to be a distance between theory and actuality. A measurable distance. We will need to bring this breach of etiquette to Lady Sigourney, as no one should know we are here," he said darkly. "Though it would be good to also pursue our own investigation into the origin of the attack."

~~~

A knock at the door startled both of them. It came again, with a note of some hesitance.

"Would an attacker knock?" Mira asked.

"I do not think so. But wait. Allow me to answer the door," Edward responded.

"That may be wisdom", she allowed. "These are my grandmother's rooms. I think I should answer. However, please do come with me."

He nodded agreement, though she could see he chafed at her decision.

At the door, a tall beautiful Willowyn, a talisma tree spirit, stood behind a laden tea cart. Its gender was neutral, neither female nor male but partaking of both. The subtle green whorls of color on its cheeks and hands were repeated on forehead and feet. Silver green moss and fronds of leaves subtly twined around limbs that blended from bark to skin and back again. A linen tunic was woven with strands of tiny silver leaves, creating an organic design that would look at home on a fashion runway. Textured, woven silk seemed to be incorporated into the tunic in shades of muted rust and gold. Some of the strands were thicker than others, revealing natural variations in the colors, with little obvious repetition of patterns.

The still form of the Willowyn was the antithesis of the storm that they had just experienced. Its form exuded green tranquility, a corona effect that rippled out and touched Mira in a way she normally associated with deep connection in relationships. A calm eddy of energy washed over her.

sister spirit sighed the Rede.

To you?

Yes replied the Rede.

"Please," sung the Willowyn in a breathy alto tone. "I am here with refreshments."

"You are a benison to the spirit," said Mira, breathing more slowly.

"Not all are so discerning," came the gentle reply. "May I serve you?"

Mira glanced at Edward, whose manner had also calmed and quieted considerably. His shadow seemed almost completely back to normal, or at least normal for a shape-shifted Dragon. He stepped back after a small hesitation, indicating his agreement to have the Willowyn enter the public living and entertaining rooms.

With a contained bow, it waited for the door to open fully. "I am known as Eenyas" said the tree spirit, the greeting offered courteously.

"I thank you for your use name." Mira gestured towards a group of couches near the fireplace.

Eenyas settled the low double-level cart into a convenient spot between the couches. Kneeling gracefully to one side, it seemed to pull the last of the tension from the atmosphere, breathing stillness into the currents of energy in the room. "There has been some disturbance?" asked the Willowyn quietly.

Mira and Edward glanced at each other "None that we care to mention." said Edward.

The Willowyn nodded her head, for Mira discerned a feminine aspect, in acknowledgement, and acceptance. It was their right as hosts to deny the evidence of their senses.

"Shall it please you to have some tea?" asked Eenyas.

"I would be grateful for such ease." Mira. said.

Edward settled into an oversized couch and Mira curled up in an armchair. They gratefully watched the poetic flow of motion and graceful ritual as Eenyas prepared the service, taking loose leaf tea from a canister decorated with hand-embellished paper. Hot water was poured from a samovar through a wicker and silk strainer into delicate celadon green porcelain cups. These were in turn placed on matching saucers. The ritual preparation was soothing and Mira felt much restored by it. She also noticed in passing that there were three cups on the tray.

Edward and Mira accepted the beautifully presented cups of Oolong tea, flavored with paper-thin lemon slices, and a generous dollop of wildflower honey. Small sandwiches and tiny raspberry meringues followed. They were offered, and accepted, followed by pastries with venison and currants, a wild onion tart, and a passion fruit mousse that was almost too pretty to eat.

Throughout the ceremonial service, Eenyas manner encouraged them to be in the moment and enjoy the repast. The calm of its form was the stillness of water in a forest pond, deep and quiet. A faint current of air seemed to create a timeless ambience around them, ripe with the delicious scent of fresh, green herbs. Mira felt the tension further drain from her limbs, leaving her relaxed enough that she could she thought, easily drift off into sleep. At first, when she noticed the tension departing, she was a little perturbed, but the Rede and Edward both seemed to be fine with it. She would go along with the flow and take the gift of relaxation at face value.

As she handed her cup across to Eenyas for a refill, Mira addressed the Willowyn quietly.

"Did you have occasion to visit these rooms when my grandmother lived here?"

Eenyas nodded serenely.

"The Lady so honored me," Eenyas said. "She was my sponsor in the magic of this place, of the knowledge of the library. It is a great sadness that she is not here to share with us her counsel."

"I miss her counsel also" said Mira "especially as she has entrusted me with a task."

"The forest beings were often welcome in these rooms" said the Willowyn, "honored as guest, and *kin*." At the last, the word kin held an emphasis that was more felt than heard.

Mira was starting to put the pieces together. Eenyas was an ambassador from the mysterious forest clans, close kin to Gran and also to herself, however far apart they may appear at first glance. This was no accidental meeting, but a deftly arranged opportunity to meet with a possible ally.

The offer of service was more than the surface offer of tea and cakes, as she would have noticed had they not just met with attack at the Residence in chambers that should have been respected for their neutrality. Regardless of the timing, it was a nicely nuanced offer of alignment, and perhaps, something more. The way Eenyas phrased things, she could take up the honor, and responsibility of kin, or she could take it as a broader kinship that all the Others shared to one degree or another. All beings could, if they were well-disposed, be called cousin. However, an acknowledgement of closer ties brought with it responsibilities, and perhaps alignment could become alliance.

Mira felt this moment was an inflection point. She saw the strands of possibility, but they gave her no hint as to direction. Her inner sense of correct action was awakened. It was the cusp point, where decision shapes possibility.

"You will be recognized and welcome here, while I reside in this place." affirmed Mira solemnly, making a complex sign in the hidden language with her hands. "You will be known as kishras, spirit sister, and acknowledged as kin."

"That is more than I had hoped for when I claimed the right of service today."

"You will experience trouble from that claim?" enquired Mira.

"It was my right," said Eenyas proudly. "The Lady would have no service except from the forest clans, and I insisted to the Chatelaine." Her voice lost music when she spoke of the Chatelaine, indicating some tension that Mira marked. "I insisted that I, and the forest clan, continue to have that responsibility."

"If there is any trouble," Mira paused, "please do let me know."

The moment of cusp was upon them, and Mira felt additional action necessary. She stood and walked over to the tea service, picking up a fresh cup. Pouring water, she added honey and a sprig of mint to it, holding the china delicately with both hands. Facing Eenyas, she raised the sweet water and said "I greet you kishras Eenyas." This was important, and she turned to Edward to ask for his attention. "You will witness for us?"

"It would be my pleasure." He inclined his head formally.

Mira took a ritual sip from the cup, and handed the sweet water to Eenyas, who, raising hands, reached for the vessel. If the cup was prepared by her hands and witnessed, it created a bond.

With both sets of hands holding the cup between them, Eenyas responded in the old way, "jarrah kishras" and took the cup from her hands. *tree sister* translated the Rede, sending a pulse of approval through Mira's senses. The jarrah were among the oldest of trees. Even a raging forest fire could not always burn them to the ground. They regenerated from a bola that reached deep into the earth. By naming Mira jarrah she was claimed as deep sister, a tie that could not lightly be broken.

"Jarrah kishras" Mira responded, named Eenyas similarly. The bond was made now, and claimed. Mira felt a vibration in the possibilities, along with a pulse of satisfaction from the Rede.

Possibility brought vision with it, and Mira could see the path open in front of her. She could also sense some of what was coming.

"There is some trouble with the Library?" she asked Eenyas.

"You see it kishras?" she asked. "There are guards at the door, where before, there have been none."

"Is that recent?" asked Mira.

"There was some trouble with the Council." Edward reminded her of their conversation only days ago. That's right, the Council wished to limit access to the knowledge in the Library. Without Gran to insist that the access to knowledge belonged to all, those factions in the Council may be able to prevail.

"If there is no access to the past, there is no place to stand in order to imagine the future." Mira recited. "That is the lore of the Library.'"

"Such is the lore," agreed Eenyas. "These were words said often by the Lady Astra."

"She has been saying them to me for most of my life," Mira said. "It is what led me to my own quest for knowledge, and my love of the invisible splendors."

"They have placed guards to prevent access to some sections of the library." Eenyas sounded troubled. "The Kasik Library, the Lady Astra's particular domain, is guarded as well. However," she looked meaningfully at Mira "few know that the Kasik Library is not available to the Council members either."

"I did not know that it was still so," rumbled the Dragon, sounding pleased. "They must not have been able to lift the binding."

"Binding?" she asked.

"Yes, it is thought your grandmother put it in place," Edward replied. His voice sounded a little strange, and her truth sense was alerted.

"It was not my Gran who bound the doors though, was it?"

"Well, it was, in a manner of speaking," he said, clearly amused.

"In a manner of—it was you, wasn't it?"

"Why yes, I am dismayed to be discovered." He did not sound at all repentant.

"You are enjoying this," she accused. "How did this come to pass?"

"At the request of your grandmother," Edward said. "That is part of the reason I was not present during her duel. She sent me to take care of some things for her. One of those things was to remove certain items from the outer shelves to the Kasik Library, and to bind the doors until she, or you, should tell me otherwise."

"Me? Okay, this is getting to be even more baroque." She was not happy with her Gran's machinations. "What else did you remove to the inner library, you creature of ancient malady?"

"Nothing much." He was attempting to sound innocent, but the glee bled through into his voice. "Just the Summoning bell for the Council, and the Book of Laws."

Mira imagined she looked as puzzled as she felt. It was hard to imagine that those things would cause particular consternation. The bell was ancient, and the Council used a more modern bell nowadays to summon members to Council. The Book of Laws may prove a little inconvenient if you were trying to research precedent, but should surely not be needed very often. It contained the record of decisions going back millennia, together with the rituals for creating binding resolutions.

Wait, the last struck a chord with Mira. If they wanted to cast a vote in Council on something as big as coming out to the humans, they were going to need the rituals of binding. Could that be it? Surely not. There must be other rituals in the Council chambers. Mira could not see where they would need the ones from the Great Library. Mira turned to Edward and Eenyas, raising her hands in question.

"The old summoning bell requires attendance by the leaders of all the clans, not just those in current favor. The old rule was that each clan has a seat in council. The current council is the proxy council. It has become the fashion to pretend some clans are not equal to others." Eenyas continued.

"As if the voice of some who cling to Council chambers are more important than those who live elsewhere."

"Argent claimed the Summoning Bell would ring on its own, if it were put in the right place. She did not want it disappearing, and she wanted me to take charge of ringing it to ensure all are present for any vote the Council called." Edward said.

"And the Book of Laws? Why move that as well?" Mira asked.

"That was my own idea. I wanted to make them ask for it. And the only person they can ask is the Owner of the Library, who was Argent."

"That backfired on you then..."

"Not so much," Edward replied. "Argent's letter, and the instructions she left with the Council, makes you the new Librarian."

"Wait. I thought those instructions were about replacing Gran on the Council?"

"They do that as well," he said agreeably.

"As well!" she exclaimed. "And the Library?"

"The Library has always belonged to Argent. She started it, the Kasik Library that is, long before anything else was here, long ago in the liminal time. It was ages before anyone else came to live here—at her invitation. It was a long time before she took a Council seat. She often said the seat was only to protect the interests of the Library. The Council members are appointed by Argent herself, apart from one seat per clan. The Council was always trying to get her to restrict access to some areas of the Library. She thought if she attended Council, she could head them off before they annoyed her by making regulations she would just have to go ahead and ignore. The Council was only an advisory body for the settlement here."

"And you were going to tell me this when?"

"Ahh. Now?" he asked, back in hesitant young man mode. He looked at her hesitantly.

"Stop that at once," she demanded. "You do not fool me one little bit."

"It was worth a try." He pulled himself upright, abandoned his feckless lad impersonation, and was once again a formidable presence in the room.

"Kishras. I need to tell my people of our bond." Eenyas gathered up the cups and prepared to take the tea things away. "What will you do?"

"We," she indicated Edward as well "will go sort things at the Library." Mira sounded determined. "Now would be a good time to let your clan know of our understanding."

She could feel herself getting irritated at learning of the Council's high-handedness in placing guards around Gran's Library. The knowledge was meant to be treasured and respected, but above all, it was to be shared with seekers. She and Gran were in complete agreement about that.

"But first," she looked down at her casual garb. "I will need to dress for the occasion."

"Shall we meet back here?" asked Eenyas. "Or at the Library?"

"At the Library, if you would not mind. I think we will be there for some time."

Mira looked at Edward. "Are there other Dragons likely to be here? Mira asked "It would not do to arrive looking like snack food."

40

MAKING A STATEMENT

Mira headed for her Gran's personal chambers, calculating what to wear to make the best positive impact when she arrived at the Library. She had a range of choices. She could arrive in court attire, or in her own formal wear, however, there was a particular long robe that belonged to her grandmother that would be perfect. If Gran had left it here, Mira was going to wear it. That should make a statement, she thought.

Fortunately, the robe was in the closet of formal wear in Gran's dressing room. Mira remembered Gran telling her about the layers of preparation that had gone into making it, back when Mira was in her teens. The first layer was a silk dress, in layers that draped on the bias, with a wonderful cut that allowed for free movement and big steps. She and Gran were of a height, so no adjustments would be needed.

Mira stripped down to the skin, carefully starting with the most basic levels of protection. She rubbed a lightly aromatic cream over her whole body, from the back of her neck to her heels, from her hairline, her face, neck, and all the way to her toes. Next she anointed the openings of the body, thirteen in all including eyelids, nostrils, ears, nipples, navel, urethra, clitoris, with a special elixir. It contained, among other ingredients, ancient salt, mountain spring water, and the dust of stars. Fresh underwear came next, followed by the under robe of bias cut silk.

Over this went a tabard woven with invisible charms. Tiny lights in the fabric were glow wisps, protective elemental spirits, helper spirits that moved into changing patterns as she moved. They would distract those who looked at her directly into forgetting the particulars of any spell they were trying to cast. It was one of Gran's more subtle magical devices. Mira reached out to the wisps to greet them and make a connection. They swarmed for a moment, happy thoughts tickling her, as they were happy to taste her. If she had not been one of Gran's descendants, they would likely have tried to eat her instead.

The over-robe was open down the front, with a cut reminiscent of Persian court wear. The quilted silk was the color of the night sky, with tiny crystal points sewn in the pattern of the constellations. Around the edges and the hem, were inlaid spells to make the wearer seem taller and more impressive, woven with authority and gravitas. Mira laughed at the necessity, while finding it comforting to have such easy-to-assume authority available to her hand.

She pulled talismans over her head, settling most of them below the tabard. Over the top, she placed her mother's sculptural art. Against her skin, she wore Gran's pendant, just at the level of her heart chakra. Mira brushed her hair out and then wove it into a complex pattern. She wanted her energy bound close to her body, and the weave would help her with that. A light dusting of mineral makeup gave her clear skin and eyes a subtle gilding, without being obtrusive.

On her feet went soft, suede boots, ideal for indoor wear, in a dusty bronze and blue. Her hands were free of adornment, except for a star sapphire on her left hand. Mira liked to think her hands were practical and strong. She kept her nails short, and buffed with a clear polish to give the nails some sheen. She noticed that the splinter from the big tree had closed over; there was little outward evidence of that adventure, and that was as it should be.

When she was done robing, on impulse Mira walked to the doors that led to the balcony. As she moved outside to breathe in the blossom-scented air, two ravens skirled over her head landing on the railing. The first cocked his head at her and the second flew at her face to get her attention. She only had time to widen her eyes slightly, when it veered off at the last minute, whirled mid-air in an impossible maneuver, and joined his brother. They conferred with each other in the way of raven's everywhere, talking like two bossy old companions.

"I am going to the Library" she said. "Would you like to come join me?" It was likely a ridiculous request, but she had been listening to S J Tucker songs lately, especially the song Ravens in the Library. It struck her that arriving at the library with a bunch of ravens would be disturbing to the guards, while playing to her own mischievous sense of humor.

"Caw" was the only response she got as they conferred again, and flew off.

It lightened Mira's mood to see them chattering and wheeling in the sky. Time to go. She went inside and gently closed and warded the door behind her.

Mira met Edward in the sitting room. He too, had changed clothes. He was wearing formal robes, and a fabulous, loose bronze open-fronted robe over the top. He looked less feckless young man, and more of the depth of his years showed in his eyes. Mira wondered, in passing, where he had conjured the robe from.

"I asked the raven's what they would think of joining us at the Library" she said. "We'll see what they do."

"That was well done. If they do join us, it would be interesting." She wasn't sure what he meant by that, but she thought it would also be entertaining should the ravens choose to join them. She was never quite sure if they understood her words or meanings, though she had always had the impression they did if they felt like it. They were thoroughly unlikely beings, and had always appeared just a little curious about her movements around the Residence.

The Library was not far away. It was just down the corridor, and across a covered causeway into the main Council building. As this region of the Residence experienced no appreciable weather, Mira wondered what the other residents had made of the storm and lightning that had accompanied the earlier attack on their rooms. She considered that the sound may have been confined to their rooms; it would be intriguing to see if anyone mentioned it.

As they crossed the causeway, a kindness of ravens wheeled across from the left, and into the covered causeway to fly around them. They swooped along and flew in a tight circle before flying ahead as if they were a formal vanguard. As Mira and Edward approached the doors to the library, the ravens landed on statues, urns, and door lintels. One even swooped at a guard's head before landing on the near-by pillar. She had the impression they enjoyed the reaction of the guards and were laughing at them. Mira was pleased. She used to chat with them when she was a child; she had not thought they would remember and take her suggestion of accompanying them to the library seriously. It was quite an entrance. She wondered, puckishly, if someone had been playing them that song. If not, she would need to fix that for sure.

"The library is restricted," said the guard on the right, with a serious tone. He was the more senior of the two, a ferret faced sentinel in council livery of grey with red accents and a council patch on his sleeve.

"Are you seeking to prevent entrance to the library?" Edward asked, darkly.

"Not at all," he said. "We are here to preserve the quiet of the library."

"Consider us notified of the request for quiet visitation." Mira had the thought that they were there to give the impression of keeping people out, while not actually having the authority to do so. Mira glanced at Edward meaningfully, in case she needed back up.

"Step aside" she said firmly.

Mira stepped forward and reached for the door. Just as she thought the guard, or rather council flunky, stepped out of the way. She didn't know what the ravens would make of the request, though she soon found out. As Mira stepped through the door, the ravens took flight and whirled in a vortex of black feathers to either side of her. She entered the library at the center of some double dozen ravens. They flew high, into the dome ahead and found places to roost and watch what would happen next.

"What's all this? We can't have this." A fussy sparrow of a man came forward from a desk at the side of the room. "The Library is not open for visitors."

"Not open? I see that the doors are quite open, and you are here," said Mira. "Looks open to me."

"What are these birds doing here?" He sounded quite agitated.

"Being 'ravens in the library' I expect." Mira replied, not helping at all.

"We are not encouraging visitors," he started to say. Mira noticed that he was wording his responses quite carefully, skirting the issue of who did not want visitors.

"I do not believe that is within your purview," Mira stated with authority.

"Who are you to say what is within my authority?" the little man demanded.

"This would be the designated heir of the Lady Argent Astra," Edward announced. "As this Library is available to all, at the pleasure of her grandmother, you would appear to be out of order."

"I am to see to it that no-one disturbs the Library." He was starting to sound less sure of himself.

"I appreciate your concern and your diligence," Mira said gently. "I am here now, and your services will no longer be required." She waited for him to understand that she was dismissing him.

"Please be sure to let the Council know that I will make my own arrangements for the Library." Mira gestured thanks, and silently radiated authority and implacable will to remain here in this spot until hell froze over. Looking nervously at the ravens, he clenched his hands and made a nervous grab for his coat on the back of the chair behind the desk. "Please take the guards with you on your way out." She could try to get the guards gone, though she wasn't sure if it would be as easy as asking. She would likely need to replace them with people of her own, though where she would find the right people, she did not yet know. One of the ravens cawed harshly as the annoying man left, with a resonance that sounded to Mira very much like they were laughing at his haste.

"My appreciation for your assistance," she thanked the ravens. Not unlike the song she liked, they appeared to be settling into different parts of the library. One even appeared to be peering at a book left open on a table in the Hellenic history section. Another perched on top of a stack of periodicals.

"Well, that was unexpected." Mira mused. "I wonder how long we have before someone even more irritating arrives to try to keep us away."

"I noticed that they are hesitant in their approach." Edward commented. "Or the guards would be armed, rather than simply being obstructive."

"I do not know which faction of the Council and there are many sent them here."

"I wonder if the Kasik Library is also being guarded?" Edward questioned out loud. "There should be some librarians here in this main section of the library, rather than guards."

"It has the sense of something thrown together hastily," said Mira. "I expected either more resistance, or to find the normal section librarians working as usual. Perhaps we should look in the stacks, to see if there might be some staff still there."

"I would very much like to check the binding I put on the Kasik Library doors," Edward ventured "Before anyone else arrives to notice that I am responsible for the doors being bound."

"I agree. I will stay here, and check these front sections of the library while you sally forth into the older sections of the place."

"Are you certain?" he asked.

"Yes. I have the ravens with me here, and there are things I can do to strengthen the natural protections, and to re-invoke the spells Gran wove around the place to ensure peaceful contemplation."

"I will be back soon" he said, heading through the far arch of the room into the further reaches of the library.

This front section was history and magic from the last millennia. The east wing extended far back into the mountain and contained the older works from many races. Beyond that, in the most protected section of the library were Gran's original extensive collections. Not far from here, in the west wing, were classrooms and lecture spaces, together with study carrels.

Mira remembered her Gran planning for lectures, and inviting guests from various races to come stay for a season or two, as time permitted. As Mira walked through the dusty light from the skylights and high windows, she was disturbed to find that the lecture halls were empty. She could sense that the Library itself, the energy inherent in any collection of books, was a little stagnant. Not enough people had been in to stir up the air.

As Mira moved through the sections of the library towards the stacks, she spotted books that were not yet shelved, piled up on a cart in a haphazard fashion. There were other books left out on study tables and in carrels. The overall air of neglect was pervasive. The more evidence of Council interference she found, the angrier she became. By the time she reached the stacks, her temper was sparking, and her face was tight. There would be a reckoning after this.

She picked up forlorn and abandoned books as she went, stacking them neatly on the front desk for attention later. At the desk was an old roster of staff for the library, from last season. So. It looked like the place had not been like this for long. A couple of the ravens followed her, looking with interest at everything she touched.

Where were the librarians? There ought to be at least three people here at any given time. When she lived here at the residence with Gran, there were regular classes and workshops for the residents, lectures with visiting experts, and the library itself was in full use as a place of research and study. Mira didn't think that Gran's disappearance could be the whole of it. This had the miasma of a plan gone awry, the failed remnants of a lack of forethought that was foreign to her way of thinking.

Gran had left an assistant after all, and one who should have taken charge here, or who should have seen to it that the library remained open and available to all. Mira wondered what he would have to say for himself when she got her hands on him. It was Gran's legacy that learning be available for all who made their way to the Great Library. Perhaps the Council had forgotten that they came into being to serve the Library, and not the other way around. If Mira had known what was happening here perhaps she would have made other choices and come here sooner. It was too late to do anything about what had already happened. However, it was not too late to make a start on fixing things in the library now.

As Mira reached the doorway into the stacks, that region where only a few brave souls ventured, she heard a soft rustling sound and a scuffle of feet.

"Hello?" she called. "Is anyone there?" She gentled her voice to avoid alarming whoever was hiding deeper in the archive shelves. "It is Mira, returned to the Library..." She waited, quietly, being very still, in case the sound was from someone too shy to speak. If it was someone who was here to create difficulty, she would make a different response, but she did not think so. The energy of the place felt smooth and cared for, quite unlike the more public sections of the library.

"Young Mira?" came a hesitant voice. "Is that you?" The voice quavered, and was weak with fear. A shy sleek nut brown head ventured around the edge of a shelf and disappeared again. Mira waited patiently. The head appeared, slowly, followed by a shoulder and a foot, and then the rest of the brownie's body emerged. "Salisha?" she asked with surprise.

"They made them all go away," Salisha whispered, "but I hid when they came, and the stringy one never came down here." Mira thought she was referring to the repulsive person who had greeted them when they arrived.

"That's all right. You did well to hide," soothed Mira. "I'm going to make this better" she said "and bring the people back."

"The Library is sad without people," agreed Salisha.

"Most libraries are," agreed Mira. She sat on one of the stools, to appear a little more approachable, something she'd not thought to need when she put on the very impressive robes. "Can you tell me what happened here?" It looked like it had been less than orderly, given the sturdy Salisha's fearful manner. Not much worried a brownie and got away with it, so whatever it was, it could not be good.

Salisha looked down, hesitant to speak. "It's all right, I won't tell" Mira assured her. "Gran would want me to fix things." Salisha started and stopped a couple times before drawing a deep breath to start again.

41

ERRANT SPIRITS

I t got out." she whispered breathlessly. "It was locked in with sigils and words, in a scribed crystal, bound in a box with no even sides." she gazed imploringly at Mira. "It got out when the Lady went away."

"Where did she keep it?" Mira asked, not sure she really wanted to know which "it" had gotten out. Gran kept several dangerous impulses locked away, to keep them from troubling the world. This world had been remarkably neutral, for a long time, just because Argent wished it so. Maybe if she found out where, she would find out the nature or character of the danger. Some of the things Gran bound were what Others would call daemons, and some of the things so bound were capricious spirits, born in the dust and the dark between the worlds. It may be a malevolent spirit had gotten loose, without Gran around to keep it in check. Mira had the sense that Gran kept the forgotten ones like pets, and would take them out to play with from time to time. Maybe one of them had gotten restless without her company. She just hoped the spirit had not been let loose by someone meddling with her Gran's arcane collection of artifacts. That could lead to more dire things going awry than Mira could mend.

"I can show you," Salisha said bravely. "It was in the glass case in her office." Okay, that was likely less worrisome than the spirits locked in the Kasik Library. The less dangerous spirits would be kept here in Gran's unlocked office. Salisha hovered at Mira's elbow, walking slightly behind her, as they wound their way back out of the stacks. Gran's office was right near the entrance to the stacks, its door in an odd corner where three rooms joined. Mira looked up at the lintel over the door; the gargoyle she expected was still perched in place, the tiny statue being one her mother had carved. Mira had given it to Gran after a holiday visit home one year.

"He did it, he let it out." Salisha said in a rush as Mira opened the door. This was Gran's office for greeting visitors, so the ward was not complicated.

"Who did, Salisha?"

"Justin did. He came to send everyone away, and when I came to clean up, it was like this." Salisha hovered in the doorway, clasping thin hands together. "It was that one. The blue box."

Mira could see a blue box sitting on one edge on top of the glass-fronted cabinet. The puzzle lid was open, though it looked unharmed otherwise. Unfortunately, she recognized it. No wonder the library was empty and desolate; the spirit that was free was an unquiet air being who shed worry and suspicion like a duck shed water. Not its fault that it had bad energy vibes. It was, Gran had said, so terribly lonely she did not have the heart to banish it for good. Gran would let it out for supervised excursions every now and then as its emanations did not trouble her in the slightest. Gran had even seemed to find the being oddly comforting; she said it reminded her how it felt to be like other people.

"Did it bother you?" Mira asked. "I can help you keep its thoughts away if you like." Now that Mira knew what she was sensing, she could feel the emanations of the lonely spirit.

"It is terrible," she said "whispering to me all the time. Can you please make it go away?"

"We'll see what's to be done." Mira said, not exactly agreeing.

"Here, now." She sketched a peace-calm-ease rune in the air in silver, offering it to Salisha with a nod. When Salisha put her cupped hands up to catch it, Mira breathed her energy into the rune and gently drifted it over to the brownie. It settled between her cupped palms and then into her aura. Salisha smiled as the tension left Salisha's shoulders, draining away from her completely in another breath. She straightened up and shook herself all over.

"There. That should feel better." Mira said.

"Can you tell me how long the Council has been keeping people away?" She sat in Gran's chair, looking around the room from the corners of her eyes, to see if anything else seemed out of place. Mira could see a couple of gaps in the bookshelves, though those may correspond to books on nearby desks. Mira did see a few places in the cabinet, though, where it looked like artifacts may have rested.

"They came when your grandmother did not come back that day. The swan lady came and said it was to keep things safe." Salisha turned brown eyes pleadingly to Mira. "They sent the people away so they could not make changes, but I did not go."

"Have you been here alone since then?" Mira asked. "That has been a long time now."

"Not so long for us who are old. They didn't stop people from coming all at once, just for the past couple of cycles. Until the annoying one came. He has been sending the people away when they try to come back."

"Has Justin come back here to the Library recently?"

"Not since he came to take things away." Salisha sounded vexed. "He should not be taking the Lady's things."

"I'll be having words with him, you can be sure." Mira promised.

She heard the sound of deliberate, familiar footsteps in the corridor. Salisha's ears were even better than hers. She had already came around to Mira's side of the desk, as if to hide behind her, as soon as she heard the sound in the distance.

"Don't worry," she said, "That's just my friend, Edward." She listened again, hearing more than one pair of feet.

"And it sounds like he has found someone else as well."
She looked at Salisha brightly. "Shall we go to meet them?"
Mira jumped out of the chair and headed for the door. "Do
join me."

42

MEETINGS

Edward and Jin Rael approached.

"Mira..." Edward began.

"Mira! Darling girl! You look wonderful" said Jin Rael. "Did you dress to greet me? What a thoughtful child." He glanced at Edward

"You didn't tell me she had dreamed." He turned his head from side to side, examining her from the corners of his eyes.

"I found Jin Rael," said Edward, completing his sentence.

Behind her, Salisha made a muted, unhappy sound.

"What's this? What's this? Is it Salisha? What a lovely surprise!" He turned to Mira "Did you know Salisha has been here for over a thousand years?" He exclaimed. Turning back to the brownie "What secrets those eyes have seen," his voice sounded a trifle sharp, then, some of the music leaving his tone. It caught Mira's attention, and she looked at him sharply in return. He did not like something Salisha knew, and she noticed Salisha tense a little at his presence. Jin Rael smiled at Mira conspiratorially "We will have to get her to tell us stories. She has the best of stories."

"It is kind of you to say so," Salisha said, in a constrained way. It looked like it was mutual; they were cordial, but neither appeared to like the other overly much.

"The matters we discussed were as I remembered them," Edward said with cryptic clarity. Mira understood that he referred to the Kasik Library being warded as he remembered. "I sent a couple more of the Council functionaries back to where they belonged," he continued "though I did need to convince one of them that I may have to bite him if he remained." He looked very pleased with himself.

"Come now, would you really have consumed such a poor quality meal?" Jin Rael asked. "He was hardly worthy as an appetizer." Jin Rael preened and spun around once in place. Mira remembered him doing similar things to distract her when she was a child.

"I think he must have believed you, Lord Eleison." said Jin Rael, nodding happily. "He ran away quite swiftly."

"I may indeed have bitten him," Edward said with dignity, "but I need not have swallowed."

43

DREAMING

How are your dreams?" Jin Rael peered closely at Mira, waiting for her response. "Did you dream it yet?" he asked, not giving Mira time to respond. That was the question he had been asking since she was twelve, and she had taken to giving him silly answers.

"Only in verses," she said now, making up responses "and it was green!" Mira pulled the last thought from the air, she thought, yet hadn't she dreamed green recently, in the big tree?

"Green? Really?" he peered closer. "You had the green dream?" He darted closer, looking into her eyes. "Why didn't you say so?" He looked excitedly over his shoulder at Edward. "She is dreaming the green dream."

"What do you mean?" asked Mira, curious about the different response she was getting. He had seemed to be waiting for something particular to happen in her dreams, something he had seen. Maybe that something was occurring now? Though he was bound to be cryptic about it. She had yet to get a straight answer from him about anything.

"What do you mean? I cannot tell. You said it was green. Things will start happening now," he announced, "and I've been so bored."

Mira decided to keep any more questions to herself. He would speak if he wanted to do so, and meantime she had a library to organize. Fortunately, it now looked like she had enough people who she could send out to find the librarians and a work party, to get things started.

"I need to get this place in order!" Mira wanted to throw open the inner doors that had been closed for far too long, yet cleaning and ordering would need to come first. She was also sure she had not seen the last of the interference she had been greeted with as she arrived. From the fairly low level of resistance they had met, it very much looked like someone was acting without formal Council approval. The appearance of guards, without the substance, together with only one person placed in the main library itself spoke volumes. She was also going to need to round up the spirit who was still leaking misery.

"Jin Rael, my perceptive friend," she flattered, "I am so grateful to find you here."

44

KRONOS DAY

O f course I am here my delicious bonbon!" Jin Rael exclaimed. "I enjoy the story of your becoming." He whirled in a circle, in good humor and, Mira thought, to show off the clashing colors of his robe. The magenta and purple clashed wonderfully with the turquoise and gold of the embellishments. "I am delighted to be here for the occasion of your Kronos day."

"Her Kronos day?" enquired Edward. "Really, you know this to be so?"

"Certainly. Is that not why you are here with her now?" he fluttered his hands, shaping a figure that reminded Mira of something she had forgotten.

"Wait. Kronos day?" she mused out loud.

"The first cycle of Saturn, the gate of time," breathed Salisha in awe. Salisha had been so quiet, Mira had almost forgotten she was there. Gate of time, time passing. Oh, wait. It was her birthday coming up, her twenty-eighth birthday, in just a few days. She had completely forgotten.

But Kronos day? Were they referring to her Saturn return? That was an odd name for it. Kronos was one of the Titans, and associated with Saturn, but it was the first time she had heard a twenty-eighth birthday called that. It was yet another thing for her to look up when she had a moment. At this instant, she really missed having a computer terminal handy for easy lookup. This realm was lovely, but it had no cell phone access to speak of.

Kronos she heard whispered internally. Perhaps the Rede had some information. *Not now* she said quietly. It would be just too weird to treat the Rede like a search agent. *Thank you* she added carefully. *We will talk later*.

"Is that so Mira?" Edward asked. "Do you have a birthday soon?"

"It will be my twenty-eighth birthday in a few days," she admitted. "I must admit that I do not know why that's seen as such a big deal?"

"It is the time when the children of time come into their gifts" said Jin Rael. "It is so exciting to watch, and wait, and see, what is becoming." He clapped his hands gleefully.

"I am happy to provide everyone with such entertainment," Mira said. "If there is anything you feel I should know about such a felicitous time, please," she looked at the beings around her "I would be grateful to learn."

There, that was correct and polite, though she actually felt neither of those things. Mira had a perfect horror of being a source of ridicule. She had suffered enough unfortunate

242

embarrassment with her young cousins. However, in beings of such great age, no doubt they viewed a child's first maturity as a novelty. Jin Rael, in particular, seemed to think she was a lively, if precocious, child. To be fair, from the vantage point of several millennia, she was exactly that . . . a child.

"Dear child, it is such an exciting time. You are dreaming true, yes?" he asked, taking her lack of response as agreement. "Then everything is proceeding as expected, yes?""

"Your foremother's children all pass through the gate of time, to take their place among the people." Salisha said. "It is part of her magic that they begin to dream true."

Mira did not think this was the time to tell them that she had been dreaming true since she was younger than her cousin Indi. From as long as she could remember, she would see things. It had terrified her mother when she was an infant, and both her parents had called on her Gran to help. One of the first things her grandmother had taught her was how to hide her abilities. At first it had been a game for Mira; it had soon turned into a habit and a way of life, a habit she was not ready to break.

She had friends back in the world who paid attention to astrology, and they had mentioned their own Saturn return in passing. It was, in human terms, a time to claim one's own place in the world. And she had thought herself at least half human. During a Saturn return, some people changed spiritual beliefs, got married, divorced, moved to other countries, took up or put down hobbies and responsibilities. It was held to be one of the cycles of seven, which was itself a spiritual number.

It was said that for the first seven years, a child grew into their emotional being. For the second seven years, they learned how to think, and in the third seven years, they explored their emotions. In the fourth seven years, a person explored what kind of person they wanted to become, and in that process tried many different beliefs and activities. She had read that every seven years, the cells of the body, every one, were replaced. This was one of those fascinating bits of information she kept puzzling at. How did consciousness keep going forward, the wave of the person moving along despite all the component pieces changing? Gran said that was one of the mysteries at the heart of magic. Harnessing an understanding of being and becoming led to the ability to shift form, and create new expressions of the self.

However, this was the first time she had heard anyone in the magical community refer to gifts being awakened at a similar time interval. She thought someone in her family might have mentioned it. Perhaps she had been too successful in getting them to underestimate her apprenticeship with Gran. It sounded like it was something important, this Kronos day. It surprised her that Jin Rael had been paying attention to her age this closely; it seemed unlike the Djinn to mark time so carefully. Mira was certain he had some ulterior motive for his interest.

"Is there some ceremony or action that people take around their Kronos day?" Mira asked.

"Some light candles for their genius, their natal spirit, as did the Romans," Edward offered. "Others make an offering at a place that is meaningful to their spirit. It does not matter so much the outward forms of the observance."

Salisha added her own thoughts.

"Among my people, and among the fae, the individual marks it in private, at the dawn of the day. Friends stand by later in the day to bear witness, to mark the time, so that the first glimpse of that which is becoming, entelekia, may be observed.""

"See, precious girl," Jin Rael said. "It is a splendid time."

"Fabulous." Mira said. "I will think on what you have said." She rubbed her hands briskly together and shook them, letting go of the thoughts of time, dreams and her birthday, for the moment. "However, there are some things I would like to notice, and focus on, today."

45

SPIRIT IN THE LIBRARY

Gentle beings, I wonder if you might be aware of the presence of an errant air spirit in the library," Mira carefully did not ask them to find the spirit, or to take any action. She was especially careful not to wish for anything from Jin Rael. As a Djinn, his nature was to be a being of wish magic; he could be very sensitive to how people asked him things. She was not sure how sensitive Edward would be to air elementals, however, she addressed the question to both of them equally.

"Please make it go away," Salisha pleaded. "It has been a terrible place to be, with that spirit loose."

Jin Rael peered at Mira thoughtfully. "Did a spirit free itself from its prison?" He drew himself up rigidly. "How then should any bid it return to its binding?"

"I know of this spirit," Mira said. "It is lonely, for its emanations are not pleasing to many."

"Was it originally in your Gran's office?" Edward asked. "Argent spoke of her special friends."

"Friends! She treated them as mere pets!" Jin Rael ranted. This was one of the first times Mira could recall seeing him so agitated, or in such disagreement with her Gran's actions. He seemed to have a particular reaction to the spirits being bound, or maybe to them being treated indulgently. Perhaps he had once been so bound himself? She could not ask. Asking would be a terrible affront to a Djinn. The custom of binding Djinn to force them to grant wishes was an old and cruel one, and no being wanted to be reminded of slavery, no matter how long ago it may have been in their race's past.

"If the Library is to be restored," Mira said gently but firmly "then the air spirit cannot keep making the energy of the place seem dejected and blue." She stood her ground. "I must talk with it and make an arrangement . . . an agreement," she amended, "but first, I must find it."

"I will not help to trap a spirit of air!" Jin Rael emphasized.

"I do not have a plan to entrap it," said Mira. "However, I do need to speak to it. I will be asking it to make an agreement to stop bothering people in the Library. Will that be satisfactory to you for now?"

He appeared to think about this seriously.

"For now . . . if you will allow me to carry a message?"

"Yes, that would be very kind of you," Mira said. She was pleased he suggested it himself. "Please tell the gentle being that I would like to have a conversation. We can meet here in the atrium, or in my grandmother's office, as is convenient." Mira turned her attention to Salisha.

"Good Salisha," she asked kindly, "do you know how to get the librarians back here? I would like to make a start in getting the place put into order."

"I do not like to leave the Library," Salisha said. "But I have a way of contacting them."

"Whatever you think is best. Please stay where you are comfortable." Mira said. "Do you think you might assist me in restoring things here?""

"I would be happy to do anything you need," she said. The brownie was obviously relieved to have someone in charge. "I will call back the librarians."

"Edward, you are with me." Mira headed back to Gran's office to get some privacy.

46

THE LIBRARIAN'S JOURNALS

When they reached the office, Mira gratefully slouched down into a wonderfully embracing armchair. Gran's office was one of the world's comfortable places, with overstuffed armchairs, lamps powered by charms, even a cozy fireplace along one wall. The shelves in here had some of Gran's favorite books, collections of maps and papyrus, scrolls on desks weighted down with interesting stones, and research that looked to be underway. It was strange that Gran had walked away from it all without resolving some of the things-in-progress piles that Mira saw around the room.

The friendly clutter was soothing, leaving her with the impression that Gran could walk in at any moment, life having been only temporarily interrupted. However, she had the sense that would be more than wishful thinking. The messages she had received, and events that had occurred, made that clear, at least, to Mira. Gran was very unlikely to come back here, to this place. It might be that she could find her on the dream plane, or in another world, but Mira wouldn't hold her breath. It was going to be up to her to make things right. Gran would have expected nothing less.

"That was well begun," Edward said, standing over near the case of artifacts.

"I expect someone from the Council to turn up at any time," Mira confided. "They may even arrive with a writ or guards to try to take charge of the library."

"I can see that you will not allow that to happen," he responded. "I will stand with you, whatever action you determine."

"My thanks," Mira said gratefully. "I am curious. Where did you find our Jin Rael?"

"That was the most curious thing," he mused. "I was checking on the binding at the door of the Kasik Library, after sending the guards away. When I turned around from the door, there he was. He must have just arrived. I do not think I overlooked him when I arrived at the doors."

"Not at the entrance to the Library, but at the Kasik? I wonder where Jin Rael entered the library? It would be good to know if there is another entrance."

"I am not aware of another entrance. If I might suggest, looking through Argent's journals may be a good place to start." He waved at the shelves next to the desk. On them were a set of cloth and leather bound books, with no titles along the spines. "I think those are her personal journals there."

"Really? Could you pass me one of the earliest ones? Let's see if they mention the architecture of this place."

"We might look at the maps as well?" Edward handed Mira a couple of journals and motioned towards a set of drawers with a map on top.

"Look at this." He picked up the map that was on top of the chest of shallow drawers. "It appears to be a map of this geographical area, across the various worlds."

"This room is a treasure trove. Let's not get too distracted by the pretty things," Mira said. He looked a little affronted. It was a truism that dragons tended to be captivated by shiny objects. She smiled at Edward, unrepentantly. "Journals first."

Edward paused near the bookcase, asking "Is it all right with you if I look at them as well?"

"Sure. It will go faster with both of us searching." Mira opened the first volume to see what they were getting themselves into. "Oh, good, Sanskrit. I can read this." Mira had a smattering of the old languages, but Sanskrit happened to be one she was fluent in. Gran was being convenient, for once. The journals might have as easily been written in Linear A or B, or gods forbid, some self-created magical language, and that would have taken a bit longer to puzzle out.

"Yes, I am familiar with Sanskrit as well, though this is a classical and early variant of it." Edward agreed, quickly reading through several volumes, pausing now and then to pass along tidbits of information. Mira addressed her own set of volumes, both of them reading quickly and easily. Gran's handwriting was lovely, and easy to understand.

"Here is something," he said after a while.

"In the year of the Nineveh fall, we began work on building the new library. I decided to keep the old palace as part of the Kasik Library to give myself a private space, with my own exits and entrances. The new library will be adjacent to it. It is not clear if the advisory council I formed will be more help, or hindrance, in the building work." He looked up at Mira in enquiry.

"That sounds like the Council was something Gran set up to help with the new building projects she had started. So, it did not start out as some kind of rule-making body for the Others?" Mira asked.

"That is my recollection of its origin," Edward said. "Argent needed people to manage the building works, and she wanted to relocate people from your world who were in the middle of the battle zones during the unrest. I was busy with other things at that time, but Argent did come to see me, in my own time and place. It was during the troubles that she asked me to teach the young ones here. She was gathering a community she said, after the wars," Edward said.

"If she kept the old palace as part of the Kasik Library, then there may be entrances and exits inside. I wonder," Mira mused aloud. "Did Jin Rael come in the same way we arrived, or from the structure that was the old palace? There may be other exits from the old palace here in this section of the library."

"I did not think to check the doors for someone coming through from the inside. The way I bound the doors to the Kasik Library was against someone entering that place from this side." He looked very thoughtful at this realization. "Is it important?"

"I do not know," she said. "However it might be important later. Let me think on it."

Edward handed her the journal, to read for herself.

Gran's hand was easy to read for Mira as she had seen it for most of her life. However, this script was old and she tilted it to put the full light of a mage lamp on the pages.

"I do not think much of the adults," Gran's journal continued. "But for the sake of the next generation, I need to save as many as I can. I only hope they will not get too much underfoot. I have had only my own company, and that of a few visitors for a while now, and will need to remember how to deal with the childish tantrums of adults who should know better. Already they are complaining that they do not have the servants and the comforts of their palaces. They should be more careful, else I'll need to cull the worst of them." Fascinating reading Mira thought. It brought to mind the immediacy of events from human ages ago. She continued to skip ahead in the text, reading an observation now and then.

"Arranged for the forest clan to find a place here. They are among my oldest allies," Mira read. Good. She had made the right move with Eenyas earlier.

"Shall I see where Jin Rael has gotten to?" he asked.

"Would you? And if Salisha is back, I wonder if we might rustle up some tea." She looked a little sheepish at the last, "I'm going to make use of the facilities."

47

PREPARATIONS

Mira was grateful Gran had installed a modern bath-room adjacent to her office. She made use of it, cu-rious how Gran had managed to get plumbing and electric lights installed in a place that usually balked at her world's conveniences. Another pocket universe? Nothing much would surprise her at this point.

There was a thoroughly up-to-date shower, sink with makeup mirror, and a bidet tucked into a corner. There was an intriguing set of cabinets against the far wall, including a long panel that looked like it could hide entry to another room. Mira checked her appearance, erasing the signs of her recent sprawl in the chair.

Edward soon returned with Salisha in tow.

"There's a delegation headed this way" he said. "They look convinced of their own importance."

"I am certain we can disabuse them of that!" Mira said emphatically. "Let's do."

"Salisha, how does one request refreshments?" she asked simply. "I would be so glad of a cup of tea. I am sure you would be pleased for a cup as well, Edward. And Jin Rael should be back with us soon."

"There is a speaking charm on the desk, shaped like a leaf," Salisha said.

"Are you going to offer those people service?" Edward asked, phrasing his question delicately.

"Not at all." Mira said. "I do not expect they will be here long enough to be offered more than the door."

48

THE DELEGATION

The loud calling of the ravens heralded the approach of the small party at the library door. The fussy man who had greeted them was trailing behind the more imposing figures of a man and woman in Council robes, accompanied by the chatelaine, Lady Sigourney.

"Oh good, Lady Sigourney, there you are." Mira calculated rapidly in her head, looking ahead to tease out the possibilities. "May I trouble you to arrange for some refreshments for six? Some tea and a light repast would be excellent." She smiled innocently in the Chatelaine's direction, ignoring the slight tension in the woman's slender frame. "It was so kind of you to help the lovely Eenyas join us earlier."

"Look here!" said the tall man in formal Council robes. "The Library is not a place for dining."

"Did my Gran not enjoy tea right here in her office every afternoon? I am sure I recall Others joining her?" she enquired, mildly.

"That's not the point!" he blustered. "The library is closed."

"The library," Mira said firmly "will be restored to its usual operations and will be open to all."

"But it's closed," said the annoying man. Mira realized she neither knew, nor cared, what his name was. He would not be given any position in the library from now on.

"Not to me, surely?" Mira narrowed her eyes. "I am certain," she stressed the word, "that Gran left instructions and messages."

"Yes, but we did not think you would..."

"Ssst. Hush." The Chatelaine silenced the annoying one.

"Perhaps," Mira rather thought they had been stalling deliberately, "you were intending to contact me about taking my position here?" Mira enquired. She kept her voice to a still, calm, and even tone, verging on being glacially polite. For Mira, when she got quiet and political, that meant she was truly irritated.

"Your position..." Lady Sigourney started to say.

Edward cut across her speech with an abrupt gesture and a wave of energy, interrupting the Chatelaine.

"Lady Miranda Ambrose Argent," Edward bowed his head formally to Mira before looking back at the assembled group. "Lady Argent is the official successor to the Council position held by Argent Astra, with all assigns and proxies."

He paused for emphasis. "She is the heir of her body, her acknowledged apprentice, and" his voice boomed "She is the Librarian."

Mira stopped her eyebrows from raising at his tone with some effort. This was not the mild, diffident young companion of the past few days, but rather a force to be reckoned with.

"The Lady Argent honored me as her Messenger. And you would be?" This last bordered on being deliberately rude. Edward had to know perfectly well who the Council members were. He was certainly questioning their right to say anything about Gran's instructions.

"I am Lord Farhad and this is Magia Linden." He did not introduce the Chatelaine, which had to annoy her. It let Mira know that he was petty enough to hold some people in his mind as more important than others.

"From the Council," he could not help adding. Good. Edward had rattled his cookies, or whatever that metaphor was. Mira could not recall at present what the saying was supposed to be; she was having far too much fun watching Edward's performance.

"I am pleased to meet you," Mira said. "Your care for the library is noted," she said carefully.

The Chatelaine nodded in Mira's direction and took a small summoning stone from a hidden pocket in her robe.

"Tea and afternoon repast for six in the Library please," she directed her staff. The Chatelaine nodded to Mira, waiting to see what would happen next.

"I don't want any tea," said Lord Farhad, clearly irritated at Mira's persistence in pursuing it.

"Good. I do not recall asking you to stay," Mira said. At this, he scowled at her. His scowl had all the indications of a facial gesture much practiced, and wielded with certainty.

Mira was not impressed. She favored him with a bland, somewhat bored expression.

"Come with me," he demanded, gathering up the annoying person, who had the grace to look cowed by the frown that had so little effect on the others present. Lord Farhad glared at them once more, whirled and abruptly departed, muttering to himself.

"I have been wanting to kick that man all day," the Magia Linden said, smiling broadly at Mira. "Do tell me I can stay for tea."

The Magia was an elegant woman, with graceful robes in impeccable order. Until that moment she had looked quite composed. Her smile transformed her face, making her much more approachable. Her lively character showed through with the vivacity and curiosity of a magpie. The Magia nodded to Edward.

"I wondered where you had gotten to. Do tell all," she said to him.

"Magia," he nodded back, looking less harsh than he had a moment before. "Delighted to see you here."

The Chatelaine looked like she could not decide whether to stay or go. There was something elusive in her expression, as if events were not to her liking. She appeared to be still puzzled about who Edward was as well.

"Shall I?" the Chatelaine asked.

"Please do stay and join us, if your responsibilities allow," Mira suggested.

"I really should be getting back." The chatelaine said. "Another time?"

"Certainly. Perhaps you could join me tomorrow morning here for tea, if that would suit?" Mira suggested.

"That would be agreeable," Lady Sigourney replied. She departed with the aloof air of one who is about urgent business and does not wish to be delayed.

Mira gazed after her thoughtfully. That had been odd; she had arrived as part of the party intending to move Mira from her place and had then stepped down. Maybe her motivations would become clearer when they met tomorrow for conversation. Meantime, there was tea to wait for, an errant spirit to locate, and a Magia to learn more about. There was also a collection that needed the hand of a Librarian to put to rights, but that would need to wait she thought impatiently.

"There have been mixed messages about the Library," Magia Linden said carefully. "Some say that it is haunted, as they feel distraught when they visit here. I can sense an unquiet spirit?" she asked.

"Yes, we are taking care of that shortly," Mira responded, deflecting the question slightly. "What messages have you heard about the Library?"

"That it has closed itself to visitors . . . that the Kasik Library has been bound . . . that the Rede of Trees has found a new custodian." The Mage looked slyly at Mira, "And that the library will be restricted to only those researchers who are cleared by the Council."

"That is unexpectedly, ah, enterprising, of someone to put about," Mira responded. "What do you think about these rumors, Edward?"

"Some of the rumors appear to be based in truth," he stated. "However, I sense there is some mischief among elements in the Council who wish to restrict access." He paused. "Magia Linden, I recall that you have a different view?"

"I have always held that knowledge should be accessible, though not necessarily all knowledge is safe for the uninitiated." She held up her hand as Mira was about to comment. "Though to the innocent and uninitiated, you can hide things safely in plain sight, and they will not notice what is in front of them. Some things are more dangerous to those who have the knowledge to unlock the secrets."

"So I have found." Mira agreed. "There are some books that need to be treated with care." Mira thought of the books in her shoulder bag. Those were not ones to leave around for just any curious person to find, especially those with a little magical ability. The books tended to attract attention, and there was some misinformation in the volumes that could cause a novice magician to have some misadventures.

"However," Mira continued, "any moderately competent Librarian can manage to point the right people to the more dangerous volumes, and vice versa."

"Agreed." Magia Linden said. "There is no need to restrict free access to the whole of the library for the sake of a few areas of reference that can be mediated by the collection librarians. They have the training and the responsibility to be the judge of what is appropriate."

"What is occurring that the Council," Mira mused out loud, "or rather some elements in the Council, is interfering so much now?"

"I have been on the Council for nearly as long as Argent," the Magia said. "It is a power play by those with little understanding, mostly among those who came late to the Council, and who wish to be more in control of events here."

"It is fear." Edward stated baldly. "Fear of what they do not understand."

"What do they have to fear?" Mira asked.

"Your grandmother cast a big shadow. No-one can remember a time when she was not here, at the center of things. They forget that this is her place, or they never knew how the settlement came to be here. They do not remember the debt they owe her for saving their miserable ancestor's lives. The duel surprised everyone. Not that it happened, but the terms of it, and that Argent chose to leave the world of form. It has upset their certainties."

"But Gran said they were pushing for restrictions on the Library long before that."

"Yes, but those were restrictions or safeguards they wanted, and specifically for the Kasik Library," Edward said. "They would send carefully chosen applicants to study at the library. However, they could not keep the allegiance of those people once they came under Argent's influence."

"Did they think the issue was with Gran, or with the Kasik Library?" Mira asked.

Magia Linden moved restlessly. "Both of those things, though they could not just come out and say they had an issue with your grandmother. They were much too beholden to her."

"Politics!" spat Mira. "It always comes down to politics and power." She drew breath to continue, but there was a commotion at the door. "Let's see what that is, shall we?"

~~~

It looked like everyone she had been expecting converged at once. Eenyas approached, together with a couple of her clan, a laden tea tray, and what Mira assumed were the missing librarians. The latter were clad in tunics with the library sigil embroidered on the upper right breast, a tree with some of the leaves replaced by books and scrolls. Their soft rust tunics were a welcome sight to Mira. She nodded at Eenyas and turned to the librarians.

"It is wonderful to see you back in the Library," she said.

"Thank you for permitting us to return," said the older man. "We were ashamed that we allowed ourselves to be sent away. The Lady would not be happy with us."

"I am certain she would understand," Mira said. "Let us not focus on the past, but rather start as we mean to go on." She gestured around at the books that needed shelving. "My grandmother wished me to take her place here. You may call me Mira," she continued, "and you are?"

"I am Arund," the dark haired older man said, tugging his tunic straight. He had a sturdy, quiet manner, though he was obviously a little nervous.

"And I am Elisa" the pixie woman said. Her hair and skin were subtle shades of a green that was tinged with blue, reminiscent of the forest clan's coloring, though with a bluer cast. Glancing at her hands, Mira saw the vestiges of webbing between them. She was associated, then, with the water beings who lived in the nearby lakes.

Mira addressed them both.

"Please, restore what immediate order you may, and I will meet with you in a few hours. The place will still feel odd for a short time, but together we will mend things."

The man and woman nodded understanding and moved off to put books away. Mira would talk to them later, once they had settled in. There was still a spirit to deal with and allies to greet.

SPIRIT AND PLACE

Mira turned to her other visitors, and reached out both hands to Eenyas. They clasped forearms and bent forward, touching foreheads together. "Kishras," Mira greeted her.

"Kishras," acknowledged Eenyas. She straightened, and gestured at her kin, a young stripling in shades of brown, and an older figure who looked closely related to Eenyas. The dusting of light whorls on the young one's brown cheeks looked like dusty gold freckles; too young, yet, to have the more developed shading of the elders.

The older forest kin was spare and straight, with coloring a little darker green than Eenyas, with hair that looked like a mixture of moss and dreadlocks. Mira was reminded, oddly, of characters from a Science Fiction television show, Stargate. The Forest clan looked a bit like the characters called the Nox. She thought it rather more likely though, that the Nox had been modeled by some artist who dreamed more truly than her fellows, and who caught glimpses of the forest clan when they were wandering in the human world.

"These are my cousin, Kiri," Eenyas indicated the young one, "and my aunt, Mosswen." She waited for Kiri and Mosswen to give their bows. "They would like to offer their services, to manage your domestic needs." Mira reminded herself to address the kin by name and not by apparent gender.

"Kiri," Mira bowed in return, "and Mosswen," she bowed a little more formally, shadowed with respect for Mosswen's age and experience, "I would be most grateful for your care."

"If you might key us to attend you in the residence?" Mosswen asked.

"Certainly." She had forgotten that all attendants in the residence needed a token in order to enter the rooms, as part of the residence security. "Do you have a token I can charm so you may safely enter my chambers?"

Mosswen reached into her elaborate hair and removed a wooden stick that held a portion of long hair in place. Kiri also reached into long brown locks and handed Mira a carved, double pronged hair spike made of a dark wood. Mira had not even seen it in her hair it matched the color so closely. They handed the carved sticks to Mira, who held both in her hands, admiring the craftsmanship.

"These are beautiful, and will be excellent tokens. Thank you." Mira preferred to do most of her magic privately, however, this was a bit of a test she sensed, so she would charm them here and now. Magia Linden was particularly interested in seeing what she did, as was Edward in his own way.

Mira centered her energies, then reached up her left hand to touch the token from her grandmother, resting over her heart, beneath her clothing. It warmed beneath her hand, resonating to the vibration of her Gran's star, and also with the pulse of her own heartbeat. She wove the magic of the combined essence together, and wove a cage of energy around the hair ornaments, wishing them to resonate to the same frequency. Gradually, as she breathed in the energy of the star fragment around her throat, it passed through her and charged the waiting talismans. Within a few moments, it was done.

"It is done," she said. "Wear these in my service and," she added, "know that you have call on me at need, should you hold the token and speak my name." She handed the hair ornaments back to Kiri and Mosswen, receiving their bows in return.

"Is there anything you need now?" Mosswen asked.

"I will be here at the Library for a while." Mira said. "I will not be back to my chambers until this evening."

"We will meet you there later." Mosswen agreed. She gathered young Kiri who appeared to be a little shy and departed, presumably to go to the residence wing of the complex.

Meantime, Eenyas had rolled the tea cart in the direction of Gran's office, out of the way of the bustling librarians, and away from the kindness of curious ravens who had been observing events.

"Darling girl!" Jin Rael appeared suddenly from behind a nearby pillar. "I have conveyed your message."

Mira was happy to see him back, but felt a little aggrieved at his timing. She was desperate for a cup of tea, and a snack. Her belly gurgled in agreement with her sentiment. Still, it would not do to appear less than appreciative of his efforts.

"Thank you dear one," she said gratefully. "How was the message received?"

Jin Rael looked around at the assembled group.

"Here? Are you certain?"

She considered for a moment.

"Please, everyone, go start tea without me." She gestured in the direction of the office. She nodded silently at Edward, hoping he would take charge of things for her. "I will be right there." Mira waited for the small gathering to head for the office, and walked with Jin Rael, away from the interested librarians and ravens.

As they reached a side room filled with books about curse tablets, she turned to Jin Rael. She hoped the contents of the room were not an indication that the conversation would become difficult.

"There. We are alone," Mira said.

"Well done, my clever girl."

"Can you tell me about your conversation with our lamentable air spirit?" Mira asked.

"He is sorry to be a nuisance, and asks if you are very angry with him?" Jin Rael asked.

"Not at all, dear one," Mira said. "I wonder if he might consent to chat with me."

"He said he would come at dusk, if that would suit you?" Jin Rael said. "Though he wanted me to be there as well."

"I would be fine with that arrangement," Mria agreed. "It is just a chat. Can we meet in Gran's office at dusk?"

"He suggested the air garden, on the nearby terrace," He offered. "Less chance of being confined."

"Very well. Though I am none too happy at the implied mistrust." The last was addressed as much to Jin Rael as to the absent spirit.

"I will let him know. Shall I return for tea, my precious?" Jin Rael asked.

"Of course, I would be devastated to deny you such a small pleasure," she said. He grinned at her broadly, all teeth and insouciant malice, and dissolved in front of her eyes, his smile the last thing to depart.

"You're not a bloody Cheshire Cat!" She muttered under her breath, careful not to be heard. She stalked off in search of tea, more than ready for a bit of comfort in what was being a very challenging day.

50

NOW WE ARE SIX

C alm* she heard the thought from the Rede. *Remember to breathe*

That's just what she needed, Mira thought rebelliously. A word in her ear, a Rede in her body, or was that her brain. Both? It was confusing. She rubbed the rune inked on her solar plexus, just below her breast bone. She could swear it itched now and then, just to remind her that it was there, though the ink was magically applied and had required no healing at the time it was wished into being over five years ago.

She must admit the day's events were making her a little cranky. Though getting miffed with the Rede for reminding her of the wisdom of calm was not exactly sensible. She was getting tired of being sensible though; there were days when a bloody good tantrum would be a relief from all this nice polite banter. Caution, she reminded herself. The beings waiting for her were, none of them, likely to be amused by a fit of childish temper. They were powerful beings who were on the way to being allies. She had best remember the lessons about etiquette or she would be causing disruption and mistrust. It seemed most of her life was filled with cautions about courtesies. Mira and Gran had spent a memorable year or so in London with Mira being tutored in such things when she was a mere teenager. Some of the more earthy turns of phrase she'd heard on the streets lingered with her even now.

It had taken Mira years to learn to control her temper. As a five year old, she had come to Gran's care frustrated with how big the world was, and how little people paid attention to one small girl who wanted to be at the center of her parents' attention. Unfortunately, the lure of paint and canvas often won out. When she stayed with her father, it was the lure of power and politics that kept his attention. It was always clear to her that they loved her; they just had their own concerns, and little time to pay attention to a child who had been, at best, an unexpected interruption to their lives.

Gran, on the other hand, seemed delighted by her existence. She seemed to take rare pleasure in Mira becoming as much her own person as she could be, though she was careful to explain how politeness made it easier to slide around the concerns of others. Ah well, those were lessons from the past. She had guests and allies waiting for her.

When Mira entered the office, which she was starting to think of as her own, the chairs and a couple of small stools had been rearranged around a now-cleared map cabinet. Tea was arranged on the top of the cabinet, and looked Mira thought, delicious.

"That looks lovely," she said, heading for a red, wing-backed chair that had been left for her to one side. "Is that Lapsang Souchong I can smell?""

"Yes it is." Eenyas replied. "There is also a lovely golden Assam, and some Jasmine tea as well."

"Lapsang for me please" Mira said. It was one of her favorite teas. "And cream?" she enquired.

"Of course. I'll have that for you in a moment. Would you care for something savory or sweet to go with that?" Eenyas asked.

"Blessings on you. Something sweet please."

"Lemon tart, orange cake, or chocolate torte?"

"Chocolate sounds perfect, thank you," Mira said, accepting a cup of Lapsang Souchong that was already infused with cream. Taking a sip, she sighed with satisfaction. "Mmmmm, this is wonderful."

"We were just talking about the Council," Edward said. "I hope you don't mind that I shared what we discovered in your grandmother's journal, about circumstances when the Council was put into place?"

"There is a similar history in the Council Archives," said Magia Linden, "though most Council members spend little enough of their time in the archives." Magia Linden paused to raise her cup to Mira "They may be unaware of their own history."

"You appear to be better informed," Mira commented.

"Mages." The Magia said. "We have a tendency to read anything we can get our hands on," she said, reaching for an almond cookie. Nibbling on one edge of it, she paused to add "which is why I, personally, don't want the Kasik Library to remain sealed. Not in my own best interests." She finished the cookie and unapologetically reached for another.

"Besides, Argent and I were friends. She was a bossy old woman as am I, so we argued about just about everything from time to time," she admitted ruefully, "which I loved about her. She could, and did, argue both or all sides of a question, and didn't tend to take much of any discussion personally."

"Gran taught me that habit as well. She said only lazy people argued from a single viewpoint." Mira agreed. They grinned at each other amiably. Mira thought there was a good chance that they, too, would be friends. She could only vaguely remember the Magia from her childhood, but she did recall Gran saying that she enjoyed her company.

"The librarians appear to have made a good start on cleaning up," Mira said. "Does anyone know why so many books are out of place out there?""

"When that abominable man, Spinner, was installed here recently, he made everyone leave in the middle of the day." Linden said. "From what little I saw as we walked through the Library, it appears that he was looking for something while he had the place to himself."

"I have some ideas about that. However, the important thing is to get the library open again, and to let people know that it is open." Mira said.

"I can help with that, I think. Letting people know that is," said Magia Linden.

"That would be helpful. I think it will take a couple of days for the main library, and we will need to take steps to get the classrooms and workshops cleaned and ready for use. Do we have any visiting scholars staying at the residence?" Mira asked.

"Yes, there are one or two who have lingered," the Magia said, "though most departed when they could not reliably get access to the main library. There is also a Dragon who is living up in the hill country he comes down at sunset every few days to express his displeasure. He has been chasing off the guards at the entrance."

Edward looked interested at that. "Do you happen to know what kind of Dragon it is?"

"It is the one called the Shaolin Dragon, the red one though I do not know precisely what kind of dragon it is."

"That is all right. She is a temple dragon, and her element is wind. She and I are known to each other." Edward said, with a particularly mysterious smile.

"You didn't happen to ask her to drop by and keep an eye on things, did you?" Mira enquired, raising her eyebrow.

"Whatever makes you think I would do such a thing?" he responded, evading her question.

Mira let that comment stand. If he was going to be mysterious, she was not going to give him the satisfaction of playing twenty questions. When he mentioned the Dragon, though, a swirl of chronons slid around her ankles, one of the signs she had learned the Rede liked to give her when events were coalescing. She hadn't at first noticed these signs were from the Rede, but lately, since it had been speaking to her, she was starting to make connections. Especially between activities of the chronons and events that she could influence by using her family gift, the gift of wishing to influence events to bend to her will. Something about the Red Dragon was, or would become, important to how events would come to pass. She did not have enough information to make a guess about it yet, but she had been alerted, and would pay close attention. It might be that it was Edward's reaction to the Red Dragon that she was responding to, so he was also going to come under close scrutiny as well.

"Lovely tea," she said, beaming at everyone. "What do you say to us upsetting the Council by opening the Kasik Library again?"

"I thought the Council had closed the Kasik Library?" said Magia Linden, expressing her confusion.

"That's what they wanted you to think." Edward said. "It wouldn't do for them to admit they were locked out." He sounded quite pleased with himself, and with good reason.

"Edward?" Mira asked, raising an eyebrow at him. "Shall we tell our guests," she trailed off what she was going to say, waiting for his response.

"It would have taken a Mage to keep the council away from the Kasik Library," the Magia commented, "but no-one claims to have done it.""

"Or a Dragon," Edward suggested slyly.

"Are you saying the Red Dragon closed the Kasik Library, and then came and complained about it every day?" Linden asked. Eenyas looked from Edward to Mira and back again, and Mira could see when Eenyas realized what Mira had been asking him.

"It was you, wasn't it, Lord Eleison?" Eenyas asked Edward. It was politely done, for she had heard Mira say so earlier when they were at the Residence.

"Certainly. Argent asked me to take care of it that last day, while she was preparing for the duel with Lord Priam."

"Why do it alone?" asked Magia Linden. "I would have been happy to help."

"It was part of my agreement to tend to things, and to be her official Messenger," he said "and she was my friend, too."

"The Lady was very wise" offered Eenyas quietly and deliberately, spreading her own brand of stillness on the room's energy currents. She drew everyone's eyes to her as she engaged in the dance of tea and service, weaving the green magic of peace.

"More tea, anyone?" Eenyas asked.

Mira made a mental note that she would be wise to ensure Eenyas was present during difficult negotiations in the future. The tension that had been rising between Edward and Linden simmered down, allowing them to remember they were, if not exactly best of friends to each other, then mutual friends to her absent grandmother.

"I think this week would be a good time to open the Kasik Library to others," Mira said mischievously. "Today, I think we should please ourselves, and open it to just a few." There, that would settle things with Linden. She was already looking both pleased and excited to be included in the group that would be included in the re-opening of Gran's ancient library.

The Kasik Library contained collected wisdom from the combined races, minus of course the more ancient knowledge that was in the Rede of Trees, but only Mira knew that last detail. The existence of the ancient library resonated through the worlds, known even to mystics in the human worlds. Some even thought the Library to be sentient, though Mira thought they were confusing it with the Rede. She was prepared to find she was mistaken, as even normal libraries seemed to acquire a kind of life of their own. Who was to say that this one was an exception to that trend?

"I noticed there is tea for six?" enquired Eenyas. "Yet I count only four, five if your friend, the Djinn, returns. Ah, that would be for?"

"Lady", came the quiet voice from the door, the librarians are restoring order. "Is there anything I can do to help?"

"There you are, good Salisha. You can help best by joining us for tea."

"What a felicitous gathering. Do tell me there is tea for me!" Jin Rael exclaimed as he arrived. "I am exhausted from all this running about."

"And now we are six," Mira glanced over at Eenyas.

"And ever so clever," quipped Jin Rael. Edward's eyes widened as he recognized the poem.

They all finished the rhyme together.

"I think we'll be six forever and ever."

Laughing together, they all put their attention to the important pastime of enjoying their tea.

51

CHALLENGES TO ORDER

After tea and some small time with all present getting caught up on events, Mira thought they had delayed long enough. She was also curious to examine how Edward had warded or rather closed, the Kasik Library. It was the oldest part of the Great Library and the reason so many gathered here at this place between worlds. She would not have thought anyone other than Gran could have closed it, though apparently he had Gran's token that Mira was now wearing. Perhaps that had helped? He was, after all a Dragon and they defied all the usual rules or conventions of magic, born as they were in the chaos of the universes rubbing up against each other.

"Are we ready to make some mischief?" Mira asked, when conversation came to a temporary lull.

"Always, dear child!" Jin Rael, exclaimed. "I always enjoy a good bit of chaos." Mira thought that rather an understatement. Jin Rael was the very soul of chaos. He disliked too much order in the world.

"Certainly," Magia Linden agreed.

"Mischief?" enquired Salisha, hesitantly.

"Yes," Mira confirmed. "I'm temporarily done with being good."

Edward rumbled with the sound she was coming to learn was Dragon laughter.

Eenyas contented herself with a small smile, folding her hands to await events.

Mira sprang to her feet, smoothing down her robe.

"Who is with me, then?" Mira asked.

"I suggest we all go together," Edward ventured. "I am assuming a trip to the Kasik Library will be a good place to start?"

They quickly fell in behind Mira, making a colorful parade. Ravens swirled ahead of them as soon as it became clear which direction they were traveling. Mira waved at the librarians in passing, assuring the industrious pair that she would see them shortly. As they moved through the Library, chronons swirled around Mira's feet.

Soon commented the Rede. *Waiting will be filled.*

Mira thought that was cryptic, but so be it.

When they arrived at the Kasik Library, Mira could see that the large beaten metal doors were closed. The doorway guardians, granite carved gryphon-lion-like-beings with large claws and eagle beaks, crouched on either side of the doors. As they came closer, the eyes of the guardians seemed to swirl with color, though as stone, they should have been inert. There was, Mira thought, no expecting the usual in the current circumstances.

"Edward, their eyes?"

"Yes," he responded, "that is part of the spell on the doors. Good Jin Rael, did you notice anything in particular when you were here before?"

"Not as such, O Dragon Mage," Jin Rael replied. "Though I came through another way."

"Another way?" Mira started to ask.

"Part of history and custom for the old palace," Jin Rael responded. "Please do not concern yourself, my curious child. I will tell all later." Mira very much doubted that. It was much more likely he would continue to keep his secrets.

"Perhaps you can tell me more when we speak of dreams?" she hinted, quirking an eyebrow at him. He proceeded to look intrigued. She had avoided talking to him of dreams, and she knew he was becoming even more curious to learn if she had been true dreaming of late. Perhaps it was time to confide something in order to elicit more information from him in return.

Mira turned to Edward, gesturing at the doors.

"Is there anything you need from us, Edward?"

"Just from you, Mira. If you would be so kind as to place your hand here on the breast seal of the guardian to the right?"

Edward walked over to the guardian on the left and put his left hand on the breast seal. They were now standing about fifteen feet apart. Mira was beginning to think his dragon form was quite large indeed if he had put the spell in place by touching both marks at the same time.

"If you would all step back to the circle inlaid on the floor across the atrium, that would be prudent," he continued. "Things are going to get very loud for a few minutes."

He started chanting in what Mira recognized as an ancient Dragon tongue. Runes started to glow beneath her right hand, and under Edward's hand on the left side. Corresponding runes glowed on the door of the Kasik Library, illuminating them all in a bright chiaroscuro of light. At the end of a phrase of sonorous speaking, Edward's voice became louder, booming and echoing off the walls. Then he roared. The others flinched at the sound. A Dragon roar was something that stirred primal fears in most races, even when the Dragon in question was not trying to eat you. There was a resonant boom from the doors. The guardians also roared in a way Mira could hear inside her head, and the doors swung open, inwards. A smash of internal cymbals caused Mira to shake her head.

Yes. said the Rede.

"It is done," Edward stated seriously. "It is your right to enter first, as Librarian." He bowed and gestured her to proceed them into the Kasik Library.

Mira shook herself internally.

We enter in. Mira said to the Rede.

The mysterious light inside the library cast shadows in dim corners. As they entered, the light gradually brightened, illuminating some areas while others faded even more into shadow and darkness. It was, Mira thought irreverently, like being inside a special effects film set. But much more creepy.

Mira's gaze was drawn to the summoning bell ahead of her, a ray of light fixing it in a golden glow of presence. She darted a look at Edward in silent question.

"Yes. It does want you to pay attention to it," he said. "It has been too long since full Council was summoned, and the bell knows its purpose."

"Be that as it may," Mira commented back. "I will be thinking before acting in this particular case." Imbued and charged objects needed careful handling.

"As it should be, cautious one." Jin Rael was clearly hoping for the opposite, given his provoking tone.

"Mischief yes. Complete chaos can wait a while," Mira pronounced.

"I would like to look around," Magia Linden said hesitantly.

"Certainly. By all means, let us explore. If there are any questions, please let me know," Mira replied. She had her own explorations to make, including an inventory of a couple of hidden chambers that she was concerned the others not venture into just yet. Gran had made a point of showing them to her some years ago, and had warned her that those chambers contained the more unquiet books and scrolls. There was even, she recalled, a scroll or two outlining conversation with spirits and Djinn that she was anxious to peruse. If it didn't work out to do so today, she could always come back alone later.

The Kasik Library was known by various names in other worlds. In her own world, it was referred to as the 'Akashic Record' by the Theosophists and other occultists. It was conjectured to hold or contain materials from the libraries of every culture known to man, including the accumulated magical and arcane knowledge from the elder races. It was not really a concern to Mira if visitors came here and read of the mysteries. It was more risky if they learned of the procedural things to do with the mysteries, the ways of seeking and setting things into motion, to transform things from one shape or seeming into another.

Some of those things were merely private to the Others however, some were true secrets that needed careful stewardship. However, Mira agreed with her grandmother that it was far better to err on the side of accessibility, with some care-taking, than to deny access to those who had legitimate reasons to do research, or to scholars with an interest in the history of the Others.

"Mira, darling girl," Jin Rael said at her elbow. "What mischief shall we make?"

"I think I shall put a seeming on the doors, to make it appear as if they are still closed," Mira answered him.

"How will that be fun?" he asked. "I am sure you had better mischief in you when you were a child."

"Should I wax the floor, or grease the handles with smelly unguents then? Or trick visitors into a pocket universe of mirrors?"Mira asked.

"No. No. Though that was a fun prank when you were a sprat. I thought you might make it look like the books were missing?" Jin Rael said.

"Now that's a worthy back-up plan," Mira mused out loud. "Shall I make it appear as if spirits have taken everything, or just the things the Council members care most about? Enlighten and inspire me do, for you are the very spirit of mischief in your own self." Mira said.

"I could lurk about and cause trouble for the Council members?" Jin Rael suggested.

"Not at all, dear Jin Rael. It would never do to reveal yourself to them."

"I could be quite invisible. Please, my precious darling. Let me play in the Library?" Jin Rael pleaded.

"And how would that be helpful to my purpose? Hmmm?"

"It would keep the Council members away?" Jin Rael said.

"And haven't we just been speaking of encouraging visitors again?" Mira looked at him seriously.

"Well, yes, but I did not think you meant those people to be welcome here," he sulked.

"I would like things to return to some semblance of the order Gran fostered here." She raised her hand when it looked like he would object. "And the chaos and mischief she encouraged as well. It is not good for too much entropy to enter into a Library." Jin Rael looked mollified at this. Mira grinned to herself. She had a feeling Gran had a willing partner in the Djinn, especially in breaking up the forces that would install too much certainty.

"Let me think on it for a while," she said. "I am certain I can imagine some mischief you would be particularly suited for." He swirled, bowed, and did his disappearing act again. Complete with that bloody Cheshire Cat grin at the last.

52

SECRETS AND MYSTERIES

Mira waited until everyone had scattered to their favorite parts of the Kasik Library before approaching a blind corner around a pillar. The area was mostly in shadow, disguising her motion as she slid around the pillar to another shadowed recess. Within it was a hidden pivot that required a gesture and a phrase in Hellenic Greek to open the portal into one of the hidden rooms. Glancing around to ensure she was unobserved, Mira entered the small room. It was one of her childhood hiding places. Gran used to challenge her to find the hidden rooms as a game, though now she understood it was part of her magical training. No wonder she had become a librarian. Growing up in this place had steeped her in mystery and wonder.

The room responded to her and gradually brightened.

"Thank you," she murmured. In the corner of the tiny room was a comfortable armchair, sitting in a slightly brighter pool of light. Over the back was a light throw rug, almost in the same position it had been when she had last visited. Mira had lost track of the number of times Gran had found her curled up in the same chair, having fallen asleep in mid-study.

In this hidden room one spoke the name of the subject for research, and the room would make clear which shelf to look at to find it. Mira centered herself, quieting her mind and emotions, and settled her Chi. She allowed her spirit to find balance and resonance with the energies that resided in the secret heart of the Library.

? the Rede indicated a question.

Shhh. Wait she responded. *There are rituals to be observed*

Mira then addressed the spirit of the Kasik Library, as if it were a sentient spirit, which to her at least, it was.

"Hello dear Kasik. I have come back to visit," she ventured. "I am looking for information about the Djinn, and also about conversation with unquiet spirits." She paused to allow time for her request to be heard. It sometimes took a little while for the place to respond. Mira wondered if it would be different now that she was taking the place of Gran as Librarian, however temporarily. She had asked for two kinds of information, however, and it may take the form of more than one artifact.

I could tell you of spirits said the Rede, sounding almost sulkily.

Later she said. *We'll have a good chat later this evening* The Rede, now that it had found a voice, was becoming insistent. She was of two minds about becoming the custodian for the Rede, and had not yet decided whether that would be a good thing. Not that there was likely to be much of an option. She had the feeling the Rede was settling in for a good long stay. It was at least strongly considering the matter, if rummaging around in Mira's brain to make itself comfortable was anything to go by. The Rede was showing signs of nesting, for want of a better word. Hmmm. There would no doubt be a reckoning soon.

Meantime, she had other things to prepare and think about. Mira was looking for information about the spirits who inhabited Gran's collection. It would be best to enter discussions with the errant spirit with more complete information. She doubted Jin Rael was going to be much help there. While the Djinn was, strictly speaking, an independent being, Gran had once indicated that had not always been the case.

The race of Djinn had been around for nearly as long as Gran herself, and Mira had the sense that some had been associated with her when she collected and made the Great Library. The Kasik was the oldest part of the magic of this place.

Across the room, the third shelf from the top glowed brightly, light focusing on a place near the right hand end of the shelf. Scrolls, carved boxes, and stone tablets, rested side by side on that shelf. Mira waited to see if the light would change or move to any other place, now that the Kasik had her attention. The light dimmed and then brightened in a slow pulse, indicating that she should approach. Mira moved a ladder into place and carefully reached out for the items illuminated on the shelf. The brightest objects were an elaborately carved stone spell box and a locked scroll case.

Both magical items made an audible sound like a chime when her hand came near their resting places. Okay. It seemed like there was more than one answer. One by one, she took the items and moved them to the chair. The scroll case was not heavy to carry, though it resonated with enough old magic to overwhelm the unwary. She rested the scroll case on the small oak side table next to the chair.

The small carved stone box, however, seemed much heavier than a paperback book-sized container should be. Mira was particularly careful with it, and sat down with the box on her lap. It had a definite 'me first' feeling to it. At first glance, it appeared to be carved on each side with no seam showing where the box opened.

Soon, it seemed, answers would be within her grasp. Mira settled down to read and learn.

53

POWER OF WORDS

Mira closed the scroll after subvocalizing the commands she hoped not to need. The scroll had given her the knowledge of commanding the spirits, should she need to demand rather than negotiate a settlement. She hoped the words of command would not be necessary. They sat with an unpleasant oily taste on her tongue, with an unpleasant feeling of constriction.

She was a firm believer in dealing in honor with beings of all kinds, and had learned from Gran that, most of the time, that philosophy worked out just fine. However, being a wishborn star made Gran a substantial force to be reckoned with. Few beings were up to the task of imposing their will on Gran.

Mira was not so certain of her own strength, though Gran held it to be significant, and so she must have a backup primed and ready, should it be necessary. She would, however, prefer not to use the binding spells that were at her fingertips. She had, as part of her training, had them used on herself, and found them to be unwelcome in the extreme. Still, she told herself, better to be safe than sorry.

Mira placed the scroll and the box back on their shelf, thanking the Kasik for finding them for her perusal. Placing her palm on the wall, she took a deep breath to prepare herself for what was to come. While she did not want Jin Rael to be unhappy with her, the spells she had to ready would also have an impact on him if she needed them. Mira hoped that this would not become a big fiasco.

I can help. offered the Rede.

Not now Mira said inwardly. She thought firmly. *We will talk later this evening. I need to concentrate now.*

Mira found the others gathered at the doors, chatting with each other about old friends and new discoveries in the Kasik Library. She was pleased they were so happy with their explorations. She had mixed feelings about her own research.

"Are we ready to go?" she said brightly.

They each agreed in turn, . It had been a couple of hours since they arrived.

"I am going to talk with the librarians, and then will be here until later in the day. Please, do meet me back here in the morning. We will have much to do, and a lot put to rights."

"Mira?" Edward raised an eyebrow.

"If possible, I would like you with me, Edward. And you also, if it pleases you to linger, Jin Rael."

Mira waited until the others had departed before turning to Edward and Jin Rael.

"Shall we set a mischief on the doors to the Kasik Library, or ward the doors as they were?" she asked of them.

"A mischief. A mischief." Jin Rael seemed to vibrate in place at the prospect.

"A bit of misdirection should suffice," offered Edward.

"Can I make the doors bite them?" Jin Rael asked. "Sting them?" He raised an eyebrow and winked. "Perhaps even eat them?"

"Hmmm. What do you think, Edward?" Mira asked.

"We can put a soft ward on the doors that is tied to you, Mira, so you know if someone approaches?" Edward suggested.

Jin Rael made a rude noise, indicating his feelings.

"Perhaps." Jin Rael said.

"Maybe we can do more than one thing?" Mira said.

They turned to look at her for explanation.

"A bit of misdirection," she said. "Work with me here."

"A ward and a bit of mischief?" asked Jin Rael.

"Certainly." Mira replied. "Edward, could you take care of the soft ward? Here is a token from me to tie it to." Mira passed over a hair pick from her pocket. "And dear Jin Rael, perhaps you might like to add a sharp sting to the doors to give any who ignore the ward pause?"

"Yes, my darling girl. That would be fun." Jin Rael whirled for the doors. Mira hoped he would moderate the 'sting' to something reasonably moderate, but was so annoyed with the Council she decided they deserved whatever they got if they invaded her territory. And the Great Library, particularly the Kasik, was definitely calling to her. It felt odd to her to be so possessive especially in such a short day.

"Good thinking." Edward replied. "I will set the ward if you like."

"Thank you," she responded. "I will go catch up with the librarians and meet you in Gran's, well mine now, office."

It was past time to add some order to the Library, and it felt like her responsibility to do so.

54

INNER WORK

Mira's meeting with the collections librarians went well. They were well on their way to having the place cleared and ordered.

Mira paused to think about next steps. There was the doleful spirit to take care of. Carefully, she reminded herself. She and the Rede needed some time to come to terms, and it looked very much like she was going to take up the position Gran had left her here. There was a Dragon who was masquerading as a real boy, or man really, a mischievous imp of a Djinn, and the machinations of the Council to manage. All that was before she summoned the full Council and before her inconvenient Family arrived. It was good that she was not overwhelmed by too many topics, for the slate of decisions on her plate would give anyone pause. Well, as Gran always said, the best way over is through. She would think of just the next thing ahead of her, and allow her deep self to work on the other problems while she wasn't looking. Her deep self, or higher self, depending on your point of view, likely had a better handle on this stuff than Mira did consciously.

301

???

I wasn't thinking at you

Sigh Mira was starting to get a sense of emerging feelings from the Rede. Frankly, it felt itchy in her head. As if it were making room, stretching, making space for itself. It felt a bit like it was rummaging around in her memories and thoughts for concepts to express itself. In an odd way, it felt like a guest moving into your apartment, and rearranging the furniture to make itself more comfortable. Not exactly comfortable, though for a guest, she would put up with a fair amount of trivial rearrangement.

We'll talk soon. I promise. Mira said. *When we get back to the residence rooms, and there is some quiet.*

**Mmmmmmmmm* Mira could almost hear a kind of agreement from the Rede, like a murmur in the back of her head. Good. The spirit, and dealing with Jin Rael about the spirit, was going to take most of her attention for the next little while.

Mira centered her thoughts on the spirit knowledge she had re-acquainted herself with in the Kasik Library, bringing her shields to the fore, ready to invoke at a moment's notice.

She sat quietly in her grandmother's chair, wondering if Gran had done similar things before her own interactions with the spirits. Or was she enough of a power to need little preparation? Mira guessed that speculation was something she would not necessarily be able to resolve. Not unless Gran reappeared some time.

She waited for Jin Rael to come back, as he had promised to accompany her to talk with the spirit. Meantime, Mira settled back into the plushness of the chair and took comfort in the familiar surroundings.

55

MISCHIEF AND MALADY

Darling. I have been enterprising on your behalf!" Jin Rael appeared before her in a swirl of energy.

"Oh?" Mira said. "Do tell."

"The doors are tricked. The floor is made subtle with apprehension. And the corridor is entangled in dread," Jin Rael said.

"Fantastic, dear one!" Mira exclaimed. "You have indeed been enterprising."

"The Dragon didn't let me make the doors eat them."

"Oh. Well. He would likely prefer to eat any intruders himself," Mira replied.

"Ahhhh, I did not think of that," Jin Rael offered. "Are you making sure he has snacks?"

"Not as such," Mira said. "Though if Council members annoy me, I may reconsider." She was beginning to feel her way. However she was not going to be a pushover, if that was what they were expecting from someone so young in years.

"Fierce you are," Jin Rael responded approvingly. "I approve."

"So, shall we go meet this errant spirit together?" Mira asked.

"Certainly. He will meet us on the Terrace."

"So you said. Well, lead on mischievous one. I shall be guided by your experience should the spirit prove difficult," Mira replied.

A short time later they found themselves approaching the Terrace. Mira could feel that the spirit was skulking around in the foliage below the flower beds. There was a miasma of dread accompanying it.

"Hello?" Mira called out in a friendly manner.

"Do make yourself known," Jin Rael said.

A fog rose up around them, together with a feeling of gloom and despair.

"What's this then?" Jin Rael said. "You promised to come ready to talk with the Librarian."

The feeling of foreboding increased, pressing against her emotions. She felt surprised that it didn't bother her all too much.

The feeling was depressing. However, it was clearly not her own feeling, and belonged firmly to another. She was okay with that, though her empathic sense was aroused. She wondered if she could help, but that was likely the trap the spirit wanted. Maybe it fed on kindred feelings in some way?

"Please. Show yourself," Mira said.

The fog dissipated slowly. In front of her was a small, purse-sized cloud, faintly blue and sparkling with thousands of tiny bright lights.

"You are so pretty," Mira said. "Why so sad?"

"No-one likes to have me around," it said.

"Well I think you are beautiful. And dramatic."

"You do?" it asked hopefully. There was a hint of pleasure in its tone.

"Yes, indeed."

"You're just saying that to get me back in the box..."

"Not at all. You don't have to go back in the box if you don't want to."

"Now, darling girl," Jin Rael interrupted.

"It's okay, dear one. Please trust me," Mira responded.

"You cannot haunt the Library though," Mira continued. "It drives people away. Makes them sad."

"But I like living in the Library," it said. "You're not going to send me away?"

"No, of course not," Mira said. "We need to arrange something that will work for both of us."

"Like the Lady?" the spirit asked.

"If you like. Though we are related, we are not the same."

"You feel a bit like her, and you called me pretty," the spirit said.

"Yes, you are a beautiful spirit," Mira reaffirmed, flattering the form floating in the air in front of her.

"If I come back to the small place, will you bring me out to talk? Can I visit with the books and the ravens?"

"Certainly, radiant one. Though not during the day. At the end of the days when the place is quieter, you could roam freely through the Library." She waited to see what it made of her proposal, hopeful that this was the arrangement Gran had made with it.

"Could I stay out here near the Terrace?"

"Yes, of course. Though I would not be able to talk with you as often," Mira said.

She waited, holding a hand up to stop Jin Rael from entering the conversation.

"Would you tell me I am beautiful?"

"I would not be able to help myself. You are easy to call beautiful."

"Well. Can I think about it?"

"Do not think too long, or I may need to give the pretty box away to another visitor."

"No!" the spirit said emphatically. "It is my chamber."

"Well yes, for now. I encourage you to think about it, and to talk with Jin Rael here before coming to a decision. I will be in the office tomorrow evening, if you care to visit." Mira agreed.

"Yes, dear spirit, let us talk," Jin Rael said.

"Though you must stay away until tomorrow evening when we meet again."

"I don't know." the spirit said.

"Do stay near," Mira said. "But not within the Library itself." She was firm in her statement. "I need the Library to become a bright and welcoming place again during the days."

"I will think on it," the spirit affirmed.

"Good. Then we will speak again tomorrow evening," Mira said.

Gradually, she saw the spirit fade and the gloomy emanations also dissipated.

"Well done, clever girl!" Jin Rael exclaimed when the spirit was gone.

"We will learn if my offer was satisfactory tomorrow," Mira said.

"Why did you not bind the blue one?" Jin Rael asked. "I can feel that you have the way of it."

"Why indeed? Should I bind a being whose only fault is a gloomy disposition? That hardly seems to be the way I wish to shape my energies. Gran did not seem to feel the need to be overly constrictive."

"Yes, dear heart. But she was a creature of astonishing Will." He paused to think. "Not that you aren't a precocious child, and full of wild power your own self."

"Having power is no reason to abuse it. Or so I have always thought. I walked away from all this for good reasons. There were those who would have sought to bind my Will before I learned to express it with my own convictions."

"I am surprised and delighted to hear you say so." He reached out to ruffle her aura. It tickled.

Mira grinned at him, glad she had not needed to use the spirit bindings. At least not yet.

"I will stay here for a while to think," Mira suggested, hoping he would take the hint.

"Dream well dear girl, when you get there," he said. "And tell me your dreams when you wake."

He dissolved, leaving the grin behind. She was almost getting accustomed to it.

56

TWILIGHT

M ira stood against the railing of the Terrace, feeling exhausted from the demands of the day.

As the gentle glow that appeared like sunlight faded, the slow dwindling light began to resemble twilight. The light moved in predictable rhythms in this pocket universe, each part being locked into a pattern of season, rhythm, and tide. In some places it was always twilight, but at the Library, the seasons most resembled those of her own familiar world. Mira thought that may have been something Gran put into place to make her more at ease when she was a child newly arrived from her own world. If so it was a generous impulse, and one that Mira appreciated.

From the North came an unexpected ribbon of dense red light, resolving into the floating figure of a Red Dragon. Jin Rael had made himself absent at the approach of the Dragon, which was a wisdom she wished she could emulate. This must be the Dragon the Magia Linden had mentioned.

Mira stood her ground, refusing to allow herself to be cowed as the Dragon came closer. She—Mira reminded herself. Though Mira wished Edward had graced her with more of a name than the Shaolin Dragon. It had the benefit of being descriptive, without being at all informative.

The light reflected off scales that glinted red, gold and then like clear crystal in the liminal light. A breeze sprang up, perfumed with alpine flowers and resinous incense. Gentle chimes and bamboo flute notes could be heard with the breeze, accompanying the Dragon as she came closer to the terrace.

Mira was entranced by the sight of the beautiful Dragon. She undulated and rippled in the breeze, impossible and graceful as no other being could be, appearing to ride the air, yet magically apart from it. Dragons, it seemed, were only faintly in the world even when they seemed most present. Some part of them remained in the chaos between worlds, forever entangled in the maelstrom that exists at the beginning of time. It was from there that Dragons drew their magic and power.

Soon enough, the Shaolin Dragon hovered in the air some twenty feet from Mira's place on the terrace. Her great head snaked back and forth, body lazily following in a constant ripple of scales and sinuous muscles. Long whiskers whipped around her head, curling in the breeze of her passage. Mira stood quite still, centering her energies and waiting for the Dragon to make her intentions clear.

Mira could hear deliberate footsteps behind her, and felt that Edward was approaching, or rather looming behind her. She did not turn her head to watch, keeping her gaze firmly on the face of the approaching Dragon. Edward was a reasonably known companion at this stage, even while enigmatic, while the Dragon in front of her demanded all her attention and focus.

The scent of incense became stronger as the Red Dragon regarded her from one eye, and then the other, weaving her head in a dizzying pattern. It was difficult to keep all of her in view as she moved.

A rumbling sigh came from Edward behind her, the tone so low that it vibrated her body right down to the bones. She popped her ears by opening her jaw, though she kept her mouth firmly closed, teeth hidden politely behind her lips.

"Greetings cousin!" he roared softly, the sound wrapping around Mira.

"Whooooooooo?" the female dragon crooned back.

"This is Mira, the child of time and stars, who is the new Librarian and inheritor of the Lady of this place."

Well that was quite the introduction, Mira thought. Child of time and stars? She would have to ask him about that epithet. The stars referred to Gran of course, but child of time? Could that be a reference to the chronons that whirled around her feet? But there, she was being distracted again.

Mira bowed formally to the Shaolin Dragon, with shades of youth-bowing-to-learned-one.

"I am delighted to make your acquaintance."

"Just sssssssooooo." The Red Dragon murmured in return.

Edward moved forward, stretching his hand out with a flame suspended over his palm. Something seemed to glint under the flame in his hand, sparkling like a handful of diamond dust. He took a deep breath, blowing gently across his palm. The glitter of particles swirled up into the fire and turned into a stream of energy towards the Red Dragon. Was this how Dragons said hello? Mira had the feeling that she was witness to something secret and mysterious.

The Red Dragon breathed in, inhaling the dust particles. She turned more transparent for a moment, scales brightened and the colors of twilight were reflected on or through her frame.

"I thank you for your watchfulness," Edward said, his sonorous voice rumbling in a register his human voice should not be able to reach. "Have you seen the wild ones?"

"Yessssss."

"Let them know that I have returned. And with Argent's child."

The Red Dragon seemed to suddenly recede, appearing in the same aspect, but rapidly swimming in the air backwards. When she was over the lake, she swam rapidly upwards in the air and disappeared into the crimson clouds.

"Argent's child?" Mira asked.

"Well, and what else would I call you?" Edward asked. "You are hers are you not?"

"Of course. I just haven't heard myself called that since I was a kid."

"And you are so old now, ancient one?" he teased her.

"Oh! You!" Mira turned around with exasperation and moved rapidly towards the causeway. It was time, and past time, for her to return to the Residence.

"May I join you?" he asked.

"I don't think I could stop you."

"That is a truth." he agreed. "Though I think I would enjoy you trying."

"I apologize." Mira said. "It has been a trying day. And I want some dinner."

"Food? Human food?" he asked wistfully.

"Yes. Human food. If I am hungry, you must be starving. Can't have you eating the Council members now can we?"

"They seem a big stringy..." he agreed.

"Not good enough for snack food." she responded, grinning at him, her mood lightening.

57

A LONG WAY FROM HOME

As she walked back to the Residence, Mira pondered the change of circumstances a few days had made in her life.

From restless dreams in an otherwise quiet life, she had been pushed into the center of conflict between factions of the Builder's Council on the world of Library. The Council was divided—between those who wanted the ability to control access to the Great Libary, and Gran's allies. In Gran's absence, ownership of the Library had become a subject of contention. In the midst of this uncertainty some of the Council had stepped in to attempt to control the Library. Mira did not agree with their actions.

Mira had abandoned the Quiet Way for the Martial Way, and had even taken up the Warrior Path to defend herself against unexpected attack. She had claimed a responsibility that she had never thought to hold, overseeing the Great Library. She had become The Librarian, though she did not know yet what trouble that would bring. With the opposition of powerful members of the Council, Mira knew she would need the support of her allies.

An ancient Dragon stood at her side, ready to act at her word. An equally powerful Djinn who had been her childhood mentor had returned to make mischief.

Many of the Others were fishing for information about the Rede of Trees, including her father and Gran's assistant, Justin. It was unclear if Justin's actions were a treasure hunt of his own or were something else. Only Mira knew that the Rede was the true Library of Time. It was the hidden lore that stretched back before language had a written form.

She had acquired potential allies and fellow conspirators, made some mischief, and had even bearded her father in his den. All things she would have taken bets against a week ago. To Mira, it suddenly seemed a long way from Seattle and the world she had built for herself since college. It appeared she was not going to be able to hold on to the planned life of comfort, nor would she be able to stay away from the reins of power.

Tomorrow was likely to bring its own troubles, including an interview with the Chatelaine, opening the Kasik Library, and making plans to put her regular life into some kind of order, and moving her cat. She had also promised the Rede that they would have some time together.

With everything that had happened, with all the strife and magical demands, her biggest dread though was the upcoming drama of introducing Dr. Horrible to the Residence. Mira was betting on the magnificent tom cat coming out on top.

AUTHOR'S NOTE

Thank you for reading Library of Time. I hope you will share your experience by reviewing the book. I would love to hear what you liked best so I can do more of that in the next story.

There are more tales to come. Mira had more to tell me about growing up with magic—you can read about that in Child of Time. Edward also wanted to tell me about how he became a real boy. For Edward's story, please join my mailing list at impishpress.com and I'll send it along as a thank you. Mira, Edward and Jin Rael will be back in a new book called the 'Rede of Trees' soon.

Thank you!
Ria Loader, January 2015

Author blog: wyrdplay.com
Publisher site: impishpress.com

RIA LOADER AUTHOR

Child of Time

Mage Apprentice (novella)*

Vanishing Dragon (short story)

Library of Time

Rede of Trees*

Author blog - wyrdplay.com

For author news and publication dates join my mailing list at http://forms.aweber.com/form/27/1997642227.htm

You can find me on Good Reads where I share what I am reading and what inspires me.

*Coming soon

www.ingramcontent.com/pod-product-compliance
Lightning Source LLC
Chambersburg PA
CBHW071230250626
47163CB00001B/124